GEORGIA RAIN

H. L. ANDERSON

Immortal Works LLC
1505 Glenrose Drive
Salt Lake City, Utah 84104
Tel: (385) 202-0116

Cover Art by Lenore Stutznegger
lenorestutz.com

ISBN 978-1-953491-64-0 (Paperback)
ASIN B0CG5CP12X (Kindle Edition)

To my beautiful sister (in-law and in my heart), Re'Nae. I'm so lucky to have gotten you as part of the deal when I married your brother! Your support and love means the world to me.

PREVIOUSLY

D r. Graves smiled as he watched Kat's perfect cast. This time, on their second fishing trip together, their target was catfish. Hopefully giant ones.

She glanced over at him and returned his smile, hers just a bit smug. "You'd better get your line out there. Remember, this is a competition."

"And what's the prize?" He quirked an eyebrow.

"Bragging rights, of course." Kat returned his raised eyebrow with one of her own, but added an adorable smirk. "Unless you had... something else...in mind."

Still unaccustomed to her open flirtation in their recent change from strictly business to post-confession of his love to her, heat rose up his neck. "I...uh..." He had no idea what to say to that. His phone buzzed in his pocket, and he turned his back to her to answer it as she laughed at his awkwardness.

"Dr. Graves," he answered.

"Dr. Graves, this is Dr. Michaels from the Georgia Department of Public Health. I could really use your expertise with a developing problem."

"What's the problem, and how can I help?"

"I'm afraid we're at the beginning stages of an epidemic. We've seen eight deaths in the last two months of young, healthy individuals stricken with severe pneumonia. Currently, in the state of Georgia, we know of ten more who are hospitalized, six of those in ICU. This is on top of a rise in pneumonia hospitalizations and deaths in high-risk individuals." Dr. Michaels cleared his throat. "I know it's the weekend, but can you come to Atlanta, Dr. Graves? Today?"

ONE

D r. Dean Graves sighed as he ended the call and pushed his phone into the front pocket of his jeans. *Well, at least it isn't another serial killer,* he thought as he turned to give Kat the bad news.

She took one look at his face and frowned. "I'll reel back in," she said before he even had a chance to tell her they had to leave.

He filled her in on the phone conversation as they packed up the gear they'd just set out.

"Pneumonia, huh?" She scrunched her eyebrows together in that endearing way she always did when trying to puzzle out a mystery. "What do you think is causing it?"

Dr. Graves hefted the camp chairs to his shoulder and bent to pick up his unused fishing pole and tackle box. "I don't have enough information yet to even begin to guess. Dr. Michaels is afraid it's the beginning of an epidemic."

After neatly fitting everything in the trunk of his compact car like a real-life game of Tetris, Dr. Graves climbed in the driver's seat and buckled his seatbelt, his hands moving liked a well-programmed robot while his thoughts spun in a hundred different directions. He pushed on the brake and turned the key in the ignition, staring out the window, but not seeing anything.

"So, what's the plan?" Kat interrupted his thought trance.

He blinked and drew in a long breath to help him return to the present reality. "I'll drop you off at your house on my way to the office —I need to grab a few things from there. Then I'll head to Atlanta; it should take about two-and-a-half hours if traffic cooperates." He only then noticed Kat shaking her head.

Her jaw set with determination, she looked him in the eyes. "You will not take me home. I'm coming with you. You might need my assistance."

Not of his own volition, his face softened as her magnetic chocolate eyes dragged him in. One corner of his mouth quirked up in a half smile, and with now purposeful movement, he brushed a stray wisp of hair from her face, his fingers skimming the soft skin of her cheek. As he thought about how far he'd come from the cold, deliberate man he'd always been, heat flushed his neck and ears. He moved his hand to the steering wheel, looked away, and cleared his throat. "Okay. Thank you. I...I'd love to have your company and your assistance."

"Damn right."

Though he wasn't looking at her, he could hear the smile in her voice.

He laughed, shaking his head, then put the car in drive and pulled out of the gravel parking area next to the river.

He stopped at home first and changed into more business-appropriate clothing, running his fingers through his relentlessly messy hair while Kat waited in the car. Worried about the long drive and possibly longer consultation ahead, he turned back and threw a few items in an overnight bag, just in case.

Kat raised an eyebrow when she spotted the bag.

As the color rose in his face, Dr. Graves stammered, "It's just in case...in case this takes a while. I don't want to drive home if it's late." He cleared his throat and avoided eye contact with her. "If...uhh...if it becomes necessary to stay the night, I'll pay for two rooms."

He risked a glance at her just in time to see her amused smile.

"I would expect nothing else, Dean. You are a gentleman to your core," Kat said.

"Umm...yes...well, thank you."

She laughed at him as he pulled out onto the street in the direction of her house.

—⟋\—

For the first hour of the drive, they rode in silence, except for the "oldies" rock station playing at a low volume. Dr. Graves silently contemplated multiple scenarios that could have been causing the outbreak Dr. Michaels described, his mind jumping from one explanation to another—all of them with flaws.

Kat closed the home screen on her phone and plopped it into the drink holder with a barely audible sigh.

Dr. Graves glanced at her and smiled sheepishly. "I'm sorry I'm not better company."

She shook her head. "It's okay. I don't mind entertaining myself, but I can tell you're racking your brain about this pneumonia conundrum. Want to tell me what you're thinking? Bounce some ideas off me?"

"Yeah," he frowned, "I should have asked Dr. Michaels more questions so I could narrow down my hypotheses."

"Like...?"

He turned the radio completely off. "Like, if he's done any cultures to determine the cause; is it bacterial? Viral? Fungal? I'm sure they've done them. They need to know how best to treat it, but even if they have done cultures, sputum cultures are not the most accurate. Sputum is hard to obtain correctly. It has to be plated quickly. Specific organisms require specific agar in order to grow..." He looked at Kat and sighed before returning his attention to the road. "Knowing what organism is causing the pneumonia would go a long way in determining how it's spreading and maybe where it started. It would at least give us an idea of where to start looking."

"What other ways are there to find the causal organism? I thought cultures were a definitive test for the most part." Kat readjusted her ponytail.

"Cultures are accurate for some body fluids—like blood and wound drainage. But not for sputum. It's hard to get an uncontaminated specimen on a living person without doing an invasive procedure."

They continued with the back and forth until they pulled into a parking garage a half block away from the Georgia State Offices building in Atlanta. Dr. Graves called Dr. Michaels' office phone, and he picked up on the first ring. "Hello, this is Dr. Michaels."

"This is Dr. Graves. We just pulled into the parking lot."

"We?"

"Uhh, yes, I...I brought my assistant with me." He looked at Kat and shrugged.

"No problem. Meet me at the front entrance."

Kat and Dr. Graves walked to the tall building and waited at the glass doors for about thirty seconds before a gray-haired man in a wrinkled lab coat swiped an ID card to let them in. He shook Dr. Graves' hand and then Kat's while introducing himself. "I'm Jason Michaels, lead Epidemiologist for the state of Georgia. Thank you for coming. Follow me."

He led them to a bank of elevators and, once inside, pushed the button for the fifteenth floor. He turned to Dr. Graves. "I'm really sorry to ask you to come all the way here on a weekend, but I really appreciate your willingness to help us figure this out." He smiled at Kat. "And you too. Thank you both."

Inside Dr. Michaels' office, he stopped in front of his desk and leaned against it, arms folded. "Have a seat, if you'd like."

Kat sat on a plush leather chair, but Dr. Graves declined the offer. "Thank you, Dr. Michaels, but it was a long drive. I think I'll stand for a moment."

"Whatever is most comfortable for you, and please call me Jason."

Dr. Graves hid a cringe at the loosening of formalities so soon, swallowed, and replied, "And you can call me Dean. I have so many questions, but it might be best to just let you fill us in first."

"Of course, Dean, Kat." He looked at them each in turn, then rubbed the stubble on his cheeks, looking exhausted. "Since I spoke to you this morning, the death count has risen by two for a total of ten deaths that we know of related to this pneumonia. The two this morning were both under the age of twenty-five.

"Patient zero, as best we have been able to determine, was a twenty-six-year-old male admitted to the hospital at Northside here in Atlanta for failed outpatient treatment of pneumonia. He went downhill fast—less than a day after diagnosis, he was in the ICU on a respirator." He looked down at his clasped hands. "They hit him with the strongest antibiotics available, transferred him to Emory University Hospital on day two. He died on day three."

"At what point did the state health department get involved?" Dr. Graves asked.

"Just yesterday, unfortunately," Jason replied. "With so many hospitals in Georgia, it took two weeks for anyone to realize there were multiple cases." He stepped around his desk and sat in his chair, folding his hands on top of the desk. "I have a feeling that as soon as the medical directors at all the hospitals get the email sent out to them late yesterday...we'll be looking into a lot more than the twenty cases we know of now."

TWO

There was only one other car at the Fulton County Medical Examiner's Center when Dr. Graves and Kat followed Jason's BMW into the parking lot.

As the three of them walked to the side of the building to the employee entrance, Jason asked, "Do you know Dr. Allen? Our head M.E.?"

Dr. Graves nodded. "Yes, Liz and I go way back. We've consulted on cases multiple times over the years."

"Well, I'm sure she'll be glad to see you today. She couldn't find an assistant to come in on their day off, so she's tackling these two on her own."

"And these are the first to receive autopsies?"

Jason nodded as he swiped his badge at the metal door. "The others were under a doctor's care and didn't seem suspicious at the time, so they didn't meet protocol. Of course, that was before we realized this may be an epidemic of some sort."

Their footsteps echoed in the quiet hallway as they walked toward the morgue; a Garth Brooks song floated from the open doorway where light spilled onto the worn tile.

"I assume at least some of the patients have had sputum cultures done. Any information on those?" Dr. Graves asked.

"Unfortunately, no. The few that were done came back inconclusive or contaminated, with the specimens being obtained after antibiotics had already been started. Gram stains have shown predominantly PMN cells, so we're ninety-percent sure we're dealing with a bacterial infection—one that is resistant to every antibiotic that's been thrown at it."

"PMN?" Kat asked as they stopped at the door to the morgue, propped open with a chair.

"Polymorphonuclear cells," Dr. Graves explained. "They are a particular subtype of leukocytes that indicate a bacterial, rather than a viral, infection."

"Chest radiographs also indicated bacterial in all of them." Jason stepped through the doorway and motioned for them to follow.

"Well, hello there, Dean. Jason." Dr. Allen held her hands up in front of her, a scalpel in her right hand. "Alexa, turn off music." Garth Brooks went silent.

"Liz," Dr. Graves said, "it's good to see you." He looked at Kat and smiled. "This is Kat Flanagan, my assistant."

"Nice to meet you, Kat. I hope you don't mind if I put you both to work."

"Not at all." Kat grabbed a lab coat hanging on a rack by the door. "How can I help?"

Liz smiled, the skin around her eyes crinkling above the N-95 mask she wore. "She's a keeper, Dean."

Dean's face turned serious as he looked at Kat again. "I know."

"I recommend that you each don an N-95 mask. They're on the shelf over there with the other PPE." She gestured with the scalpel. "We could be dealing with anything here, and I don't want to spread this bug to y'all when I open this young man up."

Dr. Graves hated N-95s. He found them difficult to breathe through. But Liz was right. They should proceed with caution. He fitted the mask over his nose and mouth, tightening the elastic straps around the back of his head. He also grabbed three non-permeable disposable gowns out of a box next to the masks, keeping one for himself and handing the others to Kat and Jason.

"Kat," Liz said as they gathered around the metal autopsy table, "you should be able to use your sign-in on our computers, since we all use the same software and server. Would you mind entering some lab orders as we proceed? I'll have Dean assist with specimen collection."

"And I suppose I'll just observe, let you know if you do something wrong," Jason said with a laugh.

"Riight." Liz rolled her eyes.

Dr. Graves put on sterile gloves and stood across from Liz.

The mood turned somber as she made the first cut. She started on the left, forming a Y-shaped incision from shoulder to shoulder, meeting at the breastbone, and extending all the way down to the pubic bone. She filled her colleagues in as she worked. "This is a twenty-three-year-old male who died this morning from ARDS brought on by pneumonia. His symptoms began six days ago. He deteriorated rapidly, was admitted to the hospital on day two, moved to the ICU later that day, intubated early morning day three. The most recent chest radiographs from the hospital showed multi-lobe—but mostly lower lobe—bilateral infiltrates that were patchy and poorly marginated."

"That's an atypical presentation." Dr. Graves frowned.

"Yeah." Liz used the scalpel to separate the muscle and tissue as she pulled back the skin. "Any suggestions on what we might be looking for would be appreciated." She laid the flap of chest skin and muscle over the deceased's face. She used the same process to pull the side flaps away from the rib cage and abdomen.

"Well," Dr. Graves said, "I know it isn't the typical presentation since the cases have come from a widespread area instead of a cluster, but have we considered Legionnaire's disease? With all you've told me"—he nodded at Jason—"about the inconclusive cultures, the gram stain, the presentation, and now the chest x-rays, I can't think of another microbe that would match up to all of these findings. Maybe mycoplasma, anthrax, avian flu—they're all hard, if not impossible, to detect too. But the more information I get, the more I'm leaning toward Legionella."

Dr. Michaels nodded, his brow furrowed in thought. "I hadn't thought of Legionella. It doesn't match up completely, but closer than anything else."

The group grew silent as Dr. Allen concentrated on removing the rib cage. She placed it on the draped table at her side and paused, looking from Dr. Graves to Dr. Michaels. "Where would the source be? It would need to be a water source. Maybe a soil source...but how do you explain the number of patients from different geographical areas?"

"That's the question that's been plaguing me as I've been trying to piece this mess together." Dr. Michaels threw his hands up in the air. "It just doesn't make sense."

"What about close contacts?" Kat asked. "If I remember correctly, Legionella doesn't spread easily from person to person—but if someone else is exposed to the same water source..."

Dr. Graves smiled, impressed, as usual, with her memory for disease processes.

"I called in one of our contact tracers this morning," Dr. Michaels said. "She wasn't able to get to her office until just before you all arrived. She should have a good start on the recent patients; the rest of the team will join the effort on Monday."

Liz finished cutting all the connections to the entire organ set and lifted the organs out of the body cavity in one bundle. She laid them on the sterile drape on the table beside her, set her scalpel on the instrument tray, and removed her gloves, explaining, "I want these samples to be as sterile as possible. Kat, can you please open some size six-and-a-half sterile gloves for me?"

Kat grabbed the package from the PPE shelf and peeled back the packaging, exposing the sterile gloves encased in paper wrapping for Dr. Allen to grasp.

As she pulled on the new gloves, Liz said, "Thank you, Kat. Now will you please put in orders for lung tissue DFA, PCR, and culture, and please add a comment that we are looking for possible Legionella bacteria? They'll need to process it differently, and the tests are technically difficult to get right."

"Dr. Michaels...uh, Jason," Dr. Graves corrected himself. "Could you contact the hospitals who are currently treating these similar patients and ask them to order urinary antigen tests? I know it only tests for one serogroup, but it is the most common one."

"Good idea. Let me make some phone calls." Dr. Michaels stepped out into the hallway.

They worked in silence, the clicking of the computer keys and the muted phone conversation from the hallway the only sounds.

—◊—

It was after six pm when they finished cleaning up. The samples had been picked up by the courier and sent to the lab. Liz had called the pathologist and stressed the importance of doing the tests correctly and quickly because lives were at stake.

They trudged to the parking lot. Dr. Graves' muscles were heavy, like he was dragging a five-hundred-pound weight behind him. He glanced at Kat and frowned. She looked pale. His stomach growled, and he cursed himself. Neither he nor Kat had eaten all day. What kind of boyfriend, or as yet to be defined relationship partner, or not *really* a relationship... He shook his head. He'd just go with "boss" for now. What kind of boss was he, to forget about feeding her all day?

He stopped and turned to her, letting Liz and Jason pass them. He reached for her hand and rubbed his thumb across the back of it. "Kat, I'm so sorry."

Her brow crinkled. "For what?"

Looking down at their hands, still in awe at the warmth that flooded him every time they touched, he said, "For not feeding you all day. I should have at least stopped for lunch. I'm—"

Kat put the index finger of her free hand on his lips, cutting him off. "Dean."

Uh-oh. She's using her stern voice, he thought.

"I'm a big girl," she continued. "If I'd have wanted to eat, I would have told you. I've been just as focused on this mysterious case as you have." She dropped her finger from his lips, to his surprised dismay. "But I am *starving* now. So let's find a place to eat."

Dean smiled and squeezed her hand. "Okay."

He hurried to where Dr. Michaels—Jason—was pulling his car key out of his pocket. "Jason?"

The gray-haired man turned to face him. "Yes?"

"We haven't eaten all day. Is there a good place nearby with quick service that you'd recommend?"

"Come to think of it," Jason said, "I haven't eaten all day, either."

Liz yelled from her car, parked a few stalls away from them, "Me either! Let's go to the Park Bar. It's laid back, good food, fast service. Shouldn't be too busy this early."

Kat laughed. Dean knew she was laughing because his idea of "early" was vastly different from most people's. It was nearing an hour past his usual dinner time. He smiled at her. "Does that sound okay?"

"Sounds perfect," she said.

THREE

The place was crowded, but the four of them found a table near the bar. Dr. Graves and Kat sat across from Liz and Jason.

An energetic waitress stopped at their table and handed out menus. "Hey, y'all, welcome to Park Bar. I'm Rachelle. What can I get y'all to drink?"

Since she was looking right at him, Dr. Graves ordered first. "I'll have a glass of water, no ice, please."

The others ordered alcoholic beverages in one form or another, and after Rachelle told them she'd be back to get their food orders, Liz looked at him and grinned. "Water, Dean? You do know we're in a bar, right?"

Jason laughed, and Kat just smiled, used to Dean's unique meal and drink proclivities.

With a quirk of one side of his mouth, Dean explained, "I neither like the taste of alcoholic beverages nor the effect on my behavior brought about by drinking."

"Ooh." Liz leaned forward, arms crossed on the table. "That sounds like a story waiting to be told."

Dean glanced quickly at Kat as heat rushed up his neck to his ears. "Ha. No. It's a story that's been long buried, never to resurface."

"Okay, now I feel like we have to know. Right, Kat?" Liz said.

"Oh, definitely." Kat shifted to face him, nodding her head.

"Uhh, Jason? A little help here?" Dean raised his eyebrows at the Epidemiologist.

Jason held up his hands in an "I surrender" signal. "These two scare me just a little. I don't dare go against them."

"Ahh, Rachelle." Dr. Graves looked up at the waitress and smiled in relief. "Perfect timing."

She winked at him and said, "I aim to please," as she set a glass of water on the table in front of him, then touched his shoulder and smiled.

The waitress set the other drinks down in front of those who'd ordered them, then pulled a notebook from her apron pocket. "Y'all ready to order?" Again, she looked at Dean first.

He nodded at Kat. "Go ahead."

She ordered some big bison burger with a bunch of extra toppings. Liz and Jason ordered next, then Rachelle turned back to Dean. "And what can I get for you?"

"I'll take your New York steak, medium-well," he said.

"You have great taste." The waitress touched his arm again, looked down at his left hand then back at his face, and smiled, letting her hand linger as she asked, "Anything else?"

"No, I...I don't think so."

As Rachelle walked away, Liz stared at Dean with her mouth open. "Does that happen often?" she asked.

He wrinkled his forehead. "What?"

Liz rolled her eyes and looked at Kat.

Kat laughed. "Yes. It happens all the time." Kat put her hand on Dean's arm and blinked exaggeratedly, a fake smile plastered on her face. "But poor Dean, here, isn't real good at picking up on flirting cues."

"Or maybe," Dean covered Kat's hand with his, "I just choose to ignore it...now."

"And by 'now'," she rushed to explain, "he means since I brought it to his attention and explained to him how women flirt."

They both put their hands back on their laps.

"Uh-huh," Dr. Michaels said, a smile tugging at his lips. "Are you two a little more than just M.E. and assistant?"

As their tablemates stared at them expectantly, Dean looked at Kat. Her eyes were wide, a panicked look on her face. They hadn't told anyone about their interactions outside of work—and while at work, they made sure to keep things purely professional.

Dean cleared his throat, smiled at Kat, and shrugged. "Maybe a little. After all, Kat is my hero." He took her hand and squeezed. "She rescued me from a psychotic killer and then helped nurse me back to health."

"Well, Kat," Liz smiled at her, "you must be very special if you've managed to catch Dean's eye. I've known him a long time and never known him to look twice at a woman, much less to openly admit to having feelings for one."

It was Kat's turn to blush. She took a sip of whatever frou-frou drink she'd ordered from the bar.

Dean's voice softened as he watched her. "She is very special." He turned to face his colleagues. "We...well, mostly me...aren't ready to make it public yet. So I'd appreciate your discretion on the matter."

"Of course," Liz said, as Jason nodded along. Her eyes softened as she looked between them. "I'm so happy for you, Dean."

All this relationship talk made him sweat. He changed the subject. "How is Matt doing these days?"

Liz brightened. "He's great! Now that both of the kids are out of the house, we're planning a trip to Hawaii for our twenty-sixth anniversary."

"That sounds fantastic," Kat said. Her grip on Dean's hand loosened a bit. She must have been uncomfortable being the topic of discussion as well.

The conversation died down when Rachelle brought their food. She asked if anyone was ready for another drink, and the three imbibers all ordered a new round. It was obvious just how hungry they all were as they dug in. The only sound for the next fifteen minutes was silverware clinking on plates and mumbled "thank yous" when the waitress brought their drinks.

Dr. Graves swallowed the last bite of steak and laid his napkin on top of the plate. Now that he could concentrate on something besides hunger, he looked around the establishment. He watched a guy at the bar order another shot of something or other, his speech mildly slurred. The guy glanced in his direction and made eye contact, frowning. Dr. Graves looked away, his chest tightening. He closed his eyes and drew in a long breath, holding it for a few seconds before letting it out.

His eyes flitted around the room, landing briefly on a table with three laughing men, then on a brooding man sitting alone at the end of the bar, then on a man and woman who appeared to be arguing—back to the bar. Dr. Graves' leg bounced up and down at warp speed, and he dragged his fingers through his hair. The tightness in his chest increased, and he knew logically that he was hyperventilating—that he was on the verge of a full-blown panic attack. But he couldn't talk himself down. His lips tingled.

Kat put her hand firmly on his bouncing knee until it stilled. Then she took both of his hands in hers and whispered, "Look at me, Dean."

His grip tightened and a fleeting thought, way back in the recesses of his mind, told him he was probably hurting Kat. But she didn't flinch. Didn't pull away. He looked into her eyes, so full of love, concern, and strength.

"Dean," her voice was low and steady, and her gaze never wavered, "take a deep breath in through your nose." She demonstrated. "Out through your mouth." Again she demonstrated.

He concentrated on the slow breaths. Let himself get lost in her dark brown eyes.

"You're safe, Dean," Kat said. "We're both safe."

Nodding, Dr. Graves closed his eyes and loosened his grip on her hands, but didn't let go. The warmth of her touch was a lifeline. He forced his thoughts to analytical mode—detailing the physiological events he knew were taking place inside his body. *The sympathetic nerve fibers in my autonomic nervous system have been activated by a perceived threat. That threat is not real. Hormones have been released from my endocrine system, causing tachycardia, perspiration, glycogenolysis. But the threat is not real. Increases in corticotropin and cortisol secretion by the adrenal cortex. The threat is not real.* His heart rate began to slow. He continued his list. *My pancreas increased glucagon secretion. My adrenal medulla increased epinephrine and norepinephrine. Blood vessel constriction, pupil dilation, increased cardiac output...* "But the threat is not real," he repeated in a whisper as he opened his eyes.

"Your color is improving," Kat said. "How do you feel?"

"Better. But now is probably a good time to leave." He pulled his hands out of her grasp and wiped them on his pants. "Sorry about the sweaty palms."

She rolled her eyes. "No need to apologize." She looked at their tablemates—Dean had almost forgotten they weren't alone—and said, "It was a pleasure to meet and work with you both. Let us know if there's anything else we can do to help."

"Dean." Liz wiped a tear out of the corner of her eye before it had a chance to fall. "I'm so sorry. I didn't think about—"

"Don't apologize." He laid his hand on her arm as it rested on the table. His voice softened. "You had no way to know... I had no way to know. This has never happened before, and I'm a bit horrified it has happened now, in front of you. It's the first time I've been inside a bar since..." He looked down and removed his hand from his friend's arm, his fingers searching for Kat's.

"I should have realized...should have picked Chucky Cheese or something," Liz joked.

Dean let out a slightly strangled laugh, still not fully recovered from the...episode. "That would have been even more frightening, I think."

The waitress appeared at the edge of the table. "Can I get you anything else? Dessert? More drinks?"

Dr. Michaels leaned forward. "Just the check, please. One check, to me."

Rachelle sorted through several receipts in her notebook.

"Dr. Mich...Jason," Dr. Graves corrected himself. "You don't have to treat."

"I don't have to. I want to." Jason took the receipt from the waitress. "You did me a great favor driving all the way here to lend your genius to this investigation. You brought up some things I hadn't thought of."

The sun made its way to the horizon as they walked to their cars. They stopped in front of Dr. Graves' car. Dr. Michaels offered his hand to him, shaking it. "Thanks again, Dean. I'll forward the results of the tests to you and keep you updated as to what the contact tracers find—and anything else I discover."

"You're welcome." Dr. Graves looked at Kat. "We'll stay in touch as well. I'm going to check with the local hospitals in Augusta to see if they've seen any cases."

Liz hugged him—then punched his arm when he stiffened at the contact. "One of these days, you'll accept a hug without cringing." She smiled at Kat. "I bet you don't cringe when Kat hugs you," she teased.

Dean chuckled and looked down at his hands. "No, I don't. But she's the only one."

Liz smiled. "Well, I'm happy for you. Stay in touch."

Kat hugged Liz and shook Jason's hand before they parted ways.

Once inside his car, Dr. Graves locked the doors and clicked his seatbelt into place. "It's getting late." His heart lurched a little when he looked up at the bar's entrance, where a tall man exited. He gripped the steering wheel and took a shaky breath. "How do you feel about staying the night in Atlanta and heading home first thing in the morning?"

"I think that's a good idea," Kat said. She laid her palm against the side of his face. "You okay?"

He loosened his vise-grip on the steering wheel and leaned into her touch, closing his eyes. "Not exactly, but I will be."

Dean started the car, but before putting it in gear he pulled his wallet out of his pocket, selected a credit card, and handed the card to Kat. "Will you please find a hotel, preferably a Marriott, and book us two rooms? I'm going to stop at that Checkers we passed earlier. I need a chocolate shake."

"You cannot still be hungry," Kat said, taking the card from him.

"Not still. Again. I think that little...episode"—he refused to call it a panic attack—"used up all the glucose just stored from the meal."

Kat searched on her phone while he waited for a clear path to pull out onto the street. He ran a hand through his hair. The traffic refused to cooperate.

Finally, there was a big enough break between cars that Dr. Graves felt safe to pull out.

Kat, apparently finding a hotel nearby, pushed "call" and put her phone up to her ear. "Hi. I'd like to get two rooms for tonight. Adjoining rooms, please." She glanced at him, then turned her attention back to giving their information to the hotel employee.

Dr. Graves stopped at a yellow, soon-to-be-red, light, wondering at her request for adjoined rooms.

With her call ended, Kat played with the phone in her lap. "The hotel is right on Peachtree. I hope it's okay that I got the rooms together. I'm just worried about you... I want to be close-by."

He took her hand, lacing his fingers through hers. He tried to smile, but the idea didn't quite make it to his lips. "Of course it's fine. Thank you for..." He shrugged, at a loss for words. "Caring. For worrying...about me. What you did back there, at the bar, I don't think anyone else could have done that for me. Grounded me. Brought me back to reality." The light turned green and, as much as he didn't want to, he released her hand—two hands on the steering wheel was safest.

His heart was getting a workout today. It bounded in his chest and throat as the warmth from touching her lingered in his fingers.

FOUR

Monday morning's alarm came much too early for Dr. Graves. Saturday night, at the hotel in Atlanta, he'd fallen asleep as soon as he'd climbed between the soft sheets. But it didn't last. He woke with a jolt not long after, tangled in sweat-soaked bedding. The nightmare had been part flashback and part incorporation of the day's events. *Carter Ridge. At the bar. Dr. Graves strapped down to the table where Kat, Liz, and Jason sat. Dr. Graves unable to move or speak, pleading with his eyes, as the Bar Killer cut into his flesh, explaining his findings as he went, just as Dr. Allen had done Saturday with the pneumonia victim.*

He leaned his head onto the tile of his shower as the hot water sprayed onto his back. He'd worried that Kat had heard him call out as he woke in the adjoining room. His jaw clenched as he struggled to extricate himself from the bedding wrapped around his body. Then, after a shower, he'd spent the rest of the night sitting on the uncomfortable loveseat in the room, watching TV with the sound barely on, not wanting to fall asleep again and risk waking Kat in the room next door.

The drive home seemed to take twice as long as the two-and-a-half hours it took in reality. Kat offered to drive after prying out of him that he hadn't slept well, but he didn't want to risk falling asleep and having another nightmare while she drove.

He toweled off and sighed. He'd hardly slept last night either. With a swipe of his towel across the misty mirror, he gazed at his reflection. The dark half-circles beneath his eyes looked almost like bruises. Monday was not starting out great.

-\/-

KAT MET him at his office door with a cup of coffee. "You look terrible. Are you getting sick?"

The right side of his mouth quirked up, and he shook his head. "Thank you for this," he tipped the cup toward her, "and I'm fine. Just haven't slept well the last couple of nights."

She frowned, creases popping up on her usually smooth forehead. "Do you want to talk about it?" She followed him into his office.

"No, well, maybe." He put the coffee on his desk and stared down at it. "Just not right now."

"Okay, well, when you're ready." She stepped around to his side of the desk and took his hand, waiting in silence until he looked at her.

The concern and steady strength he saw in her eyes made him break office protocol. He squeezed her hand, smiled, and wrapped her into a hug, kissing her forehead. He laid his cheek on the top of her head and closed his eyes, enjoying the flood of emotions that came with her reciprocal embrace. Kat jumped a little when the elevator just outside the morgue dinged, but Dean wasn't ready to let go and squeezed just a little harder until the whoosh of the automatic doors sounded down the hall and around the corner. With one last squeeze and a sigh, he released his hug, touched her cheek, then reconfigured his face into "all business" before donning a lab coat and leaving his office.

"Detective Davis, Detective Fitzpatrick." Dr. Graves nodded to them then turned his gaze to a female plainclothes officer, her badge hanging from a lanyard around her neck. "And, I'm afraid I don't recognize you."

She stepped forward and shook his hand. "I'm Detective Rodriguez, Isabella if you prefer."

"She's training with us for a couple of months before she takes old Roddy's spot after he retires," Davis explained.

"Well, Detective Rodriguez, welcome," Dr. Graves said.

"Go ahead and report on what the medics are bringing in," Fitzpatrick said to the new detective. He chuckled and added, "This is another weird one for you, doc." He looked at Rodriguez, "We told you Dr. Graves gets all the weird ones."

Dr. Graves scowled at Fitzpatrick, then turned his attention to the new detective. "I hope you don't develop the disrespect shown by these two, Detective Rodriguez. They seem to think death is a laughing matter. Go ahead with your report."

Her face remained solemn as she nodded. "We have a nineteen-year-old male, found unresponsive on the floor of the bathroom by his mother. Attempts to resuscitate by victim's step-dad and EMS were unsuccessful. Victim last seen alive entering the bathroom approximately one hour prior to discovery. Strong smell of aerosol deodorant permeated the bathroom and hallway. Nearly empty deodorant can found on the floor near the body."

"Did it appear as if he'd been huffing the aerosol?" Dr. Graves asked.

"It's hard to say," Detective Rodriguez answered. "His parents vehemently deny any illicit use. The mom stated that he"—she flipped open her small notebook and read—"'he was obsessed with smelling good and would cover his entire body in the spray at least twice a day.' His step-dad said they told him multiple times that he was using too much; they could not only smell it all the way downstairs but taste it."

Dr. Graves frowned. The group of five looked toward the elevator as it descended to the basement. Detective Davis activated the automatic glass doors into the morgue as the medics wheeled the stretcher out of the elevator. As they lifted the body bag onto the exam table, a waft of cologne-like scent blew through the room, even through the closed bag.

"Thank you." Dr. Graves nodded to the two medics then turned to the detectives. "I'll let you know when I have the official autopsy results. The toxicology report will likely take two to four weeks to get back. Detective Rodriguez, it was a pleasure to meet you."

As the elevator doors closed on the detectives and medics, Dr. Graves' shoulders slumped and he let out a deep breath. He really hated the deaths of young people. He moved to the table and unzipped the body bag. Kat handed him a pair of gloves, her hands already gloved, and they worked together in silence to remove the deceased from the bag—rolling him to one side and tucking the bag under his body, then rolling him to the other side and pulling the bag out from under him.

Kat prepared the instrument table and booted up the computer while Dr. Graves put on a gown, mask, goggles, and gloves. He tapped his foot on the switch to turn the overhead light on then positioned it so the beam aimed at the deceased's mouth and nose. He clicked the "record" button, also with his foot, and spoke loud enough that the microphone hanging from above could catch his words. "Nasal passages unremarkable. No sign of dried blood, irritation, or ulcers." He pried the young man's jaw open, and Kat handed him a bite block which he carefully inserted to keep the mouth ajar. He readjusted the light. "Oral cavity free of blood, irritation, inflammation, and ulcers. Normal-appearing mucosa."

The green light on the microphone turned red as he turned it off. He couldn't help but smile slightly as Kat began removing the deceased's clothing in preparation for the autopsy. They worked together like a well-oiled machine. *That's too cliché*, Dr. Graves thought. *We work together like Molly Weasley's kitchen magic: dishes being scrubbed, meals being prepared, and love emanating from the magical matriarch.* He glanced at Kat as the thought of love passed through his mind. He nodded to himself, proud of his much-improved analogy.

AFTER RADIOGRAPHS HAD BEEN PERFORMED and all the internal organs had been weighed, measured, and inspected, Dr. Graves started the process of suturing the incisions back together. "Send the blood samples for the usual toxicology tests and add on butane and propane levels, please."

Kat printed out the labels and carefully placed them on the specimen tubes and tissue samples. "What are you thinking happened? I assume that you don't believe he was intentionally inhaling the fumes because his mouth and nose look normal."

"Well, the official cause of death was a myocardial infarction—"

"He's so young to have had a heart attack," Kat interrupted.

"Very young. But I believe it was brought on by the extreme overuse of deodorant spray. Some of the chemicals in such sprays can be toxic at high levels."

"Tragic." Kat looked at the young man. "Is that something that happens often?"

"No, thankfully." He sighed. "Those detectives aren't wrong. I do seem to always get the unusual death cases."

—⁄\—

DR. GRAVES' desk phone rang just as he settled into his chair. "Dr. Graves," he answered, cradling the phone between his ear and shoulder.

"Hi, Dean, this is Jason Michaels."

Dr. Graves sat up straighter. "Any news?"

"A couple of things. Regarding the urinary antigen tests we asked the hospitals to run on their suspect patients—six out of ten came back positive for *Legionella*. We've sent sputum samples on all of them for cultures, but won't get those back for another day or two. With all ten patients having almost identical symptoms, I'm still betting on *Legionella* for the four negatives, just maybe a strain not detected by the antigen test." He took a deep breath.

"You sound exhausted," Dr. Graves said. "Are you getting any sleep?"

"Not much. My wife brought my camping cot to work with a blanket and pillow, and I've been catching a few winks when I can."

"Jason, you need to make sure you're taking care of yourself..." His voice faded out as he remembered his own lack of self-care when he'd been trying to find Carter Ridge before he killed again.

Dr. Michaels laughed, probably coming to the same conclusion. "Well, I should be able to slow down in a day or two."

"Anything else?"

"Yeah. I heard back from some of the hospitals we sent alerts to Saturday, and there appears to be at least three patients in your area."

"Well, crap," Dr. Graves said. "Which hospitals?"

"They're all at Augusta University. I figured I'd see if you wanted to contact them to let them know what tests to run, or if you want me to call."

"You have enough on your plate. I know the ID doctor there. I'll give him a call right now."

"Thank you, Dean. I'll let you know how those cultures turn out."

"You're welcome. Talk to you soon." Dr. Graves hung up and looked up the Infectious Disease doctor's number, picked the phone back up, and dialed.

"Hello." The thick Indian accent and failure to identify himself were key indicators that he'd reached Dr. Shah.

"Dr. Shah, Dr. Graves here. How are you doing?"

"Ahh, Dean, good to hear from you. I'm doing well. What can I help you with?"

Dr. Graves paused a few seconds to get his thoughts in order. "Well, I'm sure you've heard by now that we may have a pandemic of some sort on our hands."

"Yes. I saw the alert first thing this morning."

"I've been working with the folks in Atlanta on this, and it looks like we're dealing with some resistant, lethal strain of *Legionella*—"

Dr. Shah interrupted him. "*Legionella?* But that isn't typically fatal, especially to young people."

"I know. But, like I said, we might be dealing with something new here. The state lab is working on getting culture and sensitivities done. In the meantime, we have seen some positive UATs. My suggestion, and that of Dr. Michaels in Atlanta, is that you run a UAT on any patients that fit the criteria outlined in the alert, obtain a clean sputum sample and send it to the state lab, and," Dr. Graves sighed, "send any deceased in for an autopsy."

"Yes. Okay." Dr. Shah hummed a moment. "I'm hitting these patients with heavy-duty antibiotics. Two of them are on life support, and I anticipate the third will be by the end of the day. Any suggestions on treatment? Has anything shown promise in treating this?"

"Not yet, but we just got the confirmation that we're dealing with *Legionella*, so hopefully the treatments can be catered to that."

"Yes. Yes. I need to go write some new orders for these patients. Keep me in the loop, please, Dean. Bye." He hung up.

Dr. Graves looked at the clock and rubbed his temples. With a sigh, he picked up the phone again to call the other big hospitals in Augusta just in case the email alert had gone unnoticed and to give them the additional information and instructions.

FIVE

The hostess led them to a quiet table tucked away in the back as Dean had requested. Kat sat across from him and picked up the menu.

"Craig will be your server tonight, and he should be right with you." The young hostess smiled and hurried back to the front of the restaurant.

Dean opened the menu and gazed at it, not really focusing, not really hungry.

"Hi! I'm Craig and I'll be your server tonight. What can I get you to drink?"

Dean twitched and dropped the menu. How had he not noticed the guy walking up to their table? He glanced at Kat, hoping she hadn't seen his reaction. The worried crease of her forehead indicated that she had, though. He smiled at her then turned to Craig. "I'll have water, no ice, please."

Kat ordered a diet soda.

Craig wrote their drink orders down in his notebook. "Would you like any appetizers? Some mozzarella sticks maybe?"

"No, thank you," Kat answered.

"Okay. I'll be right back with your drinks and to take your order." He disappeared toward the kitchen.

"You okay?" Kat asked.

Dr. Graves' first inclination was to brush her concern off, conceal his distress as of late. But that would be like lying to her—and he didn't want to do that. Plus, she could clearly see he was struggling.

He sighed and ran his fingers through his hair. "Not really. I think I just need a good night's sleep."

"That would be a start," she said. "What is it that's keeping you from sleeping?"

This time, Dean saw the server approaching their table. Craig set their drinks down and pulled his notebook out of his apron pocket. "Are you ready to order?"

Kat looked at Dean and he shrugged. "You go first."

"I'll have the chicken fettuccini." She closed the menu and handed it to the server.

"And you, sir?" Craig turned to Dean.

"I'll have a Caesar salad."

As the server walked away, Kat reached across the table and squeezed Dean's hand. "Like I said earlier today, you don't have to talk about it until you're ready, but I think it might help with your sleep issues if you do."

He stared at their hands for a few seconds, his vision blurring as his mind wandered. Blinking, he focused and lifted Kat's hand to his lips, pressing them against it and savoring the warmth that flooded through him. He wrapped her hand in both of his as he lowered it to the table. "I've been having nightmares."

Kat nodded. "I think I can guess the subject matter involved."

"Huh," he chuckled. "Yes, I bet you can."

They sat in silence, Kat so attuned to what he needed even though he, himself, didn't have it figured out yet. He struggled to find the words to explain, his usually well-ordered thoughts flitting all over the place. How much should he share? How detailed should he get? Would Kat see him differently? Would she think him weak? He closed his eyes tight and bowed his head as he drew in a breath. Opening his eyes, he looked at Kat and the words fell out of him in hushed tones. "The dreams are similar, just different locations and not always the same...uhh...the same *observers*. Like in Atlanta, it was in the bar where we ate. You and Liz and Jacob were just sitting at the table. *He*, Carter, had me strapped to it and you all watched while he cut into me, explaining his...his *findings* as he went. I woke up tangled in the bedsheets and basically had an anxiety attack trying to free myself. I was..." He swallowed hard but didn't move his gaze from hers. "I was afraid to go back to sleep."

Kat bit her bottom lip but didn't say anything, letting him continue.

"Then last night, I didn't want to go to sleep, but I was so tired. This time the dream took place on my back deck." Anger flashed in his guts and burned his throat as he spat out his next words. "*My back deck!* Where I relax and paint and play with the neighbor's stupid dog! You were there again. And the dog. Winston,"—he smiled just a little—"he growled at *him.*

"The worst part—aside from you seeing me like that...again—was when I woke up, drenched in sweat, I still couldn't move. I couldn't scream. Couldn't blink. Just like..." Dean shook his head. He couldn't finish.

"Sleep paralysis." Kat's voice tremored a little and moisture filled her eyes but didn't spill over. "I've heard about that. It sounds horrible, doubly so after what you went through."

He nodded and ran a hand through his hair again. "When I could finally move, I was tangled in my sheets—I think I'll start sleeping on a bare mattress—and I panicked, again. It was only midnight, but there was no way I was going to go back to sleep. I brewed some coffee and sat at the kitchen table doing crossword puzzles until the sun came up."

"Here's your Caesar salad," Craig, the server, said in a much too enthusiastic voice.

Dr. Graves jumped in his seat and, scowling at the young man, growled, "Have you ever thought of announcing yourself before just plopping stuff down on the damn table?"

Kat removed her hand from Dean's, giving him a worried look, then smiled up at the young man still holding her large bowl of Alfredo with his mouth partially open. "Thank you, Craig. You're doing a great job. You can just set that right here." She patted the table in front of her.

What was wrong with him? Dr. Graves lowered his head, ashamed at his own behavior, and said to the server, "Craig, wait. I'm sorry I snapped at you. My jumpiness is not your fault. You've been very attentive and quick. Thank you."

"You're welcome. I'll try to remember to make some noise on my way over next time." He smiled and nodded at Dr. Graves.

A minute ago Dean couldn't move his eyes away from Kat's, now he couldn't look at her. He stirred the romaine lettuce around in the bowl but couldn't muster the appetite to take a bite. He dropped the fork, letting it clatter against the dish.

"Dean," Kat said, "you need to eat. Even if you don't feel like it. You're body needs sustenance."

Several feelings at once overwhelmed him, and he dropped his face into his hands. His throat tightened as he tried to swallow, and tears burned his eyes. She was right, he needed to eat, but how could he when guilt and fear, anger, and hopelessness all tore at his stomach like the world's biggest ulcer? He wasn't any good for Kat like this. Wasn't any good, period. He wanted to leave but couldn't muster the energy to move.

Kat's fork clanked to the table, and before he could take another ragged breath, she was sitting next to him, her arms around him, her head resting against his shoulder. Tears dripped through his fingers onto the table and he cussed silently at himself. *Pull yourself together, Dean Graves. This isn't you. This isn't who you are.* He forced himself to think analytically. *Sleep deprivation can cause drowsiness, irritability, reduced physical strength, mood swings...*

Kat lifted her head and whispered in his ear, "I love you, Dean Graves. We'll get through this together."

Those words broke through his sleep-deprived hysteria. He turned toward her and enveloped her in his arms, kissing her forehead with tear-soaked lips. Next to her ear, he whispered, "I love you too. And I'm sorry. I don't know what's gotten into me." He did know, but he shouldn't be letting it affect him like this. He should be able to explain these feelings, dreams—moods—away with facts. With reality. Why was he letting Carter Ridge into his head? The psychopath was dead, he couldn't do anything to Dean.

Someone humming *The Hills are Alive* approached their table, and Dean and Kat untangled themselves from each other. Dean wiped his face then laughed as Craig stepped up beside them. "Julie Andrews fan?" Dean asked.

"Who isn't?" Craig smiled. "Is everything okay with your food? You haven't eaten much. Can I get you something else?"

Kat answered, "No, thank you. We're going to eat in just a minute."

The server nodded and, as he walked away, hummed a pathetic version of *Spoon Full of Sugar*, causing both Kat and Dean to laugh.

Kat moved back over to her side of the table and they both ate, Dean forcing himself to swallow the small bites he took.

As they walked back to his car hand-in-hand, Kat said, "Maybe I should come stay with you for a few days. Having someone else in the house might...I don't know...help?"

Dr. Graves stiffened. Was she suggesting...? "I...umm...I'm not, uh, ready for that."

She punched his shoulder and laughed. "I'm not suggesting anything indecent, Dean. If you don't feel comfortable having *me* there, maybe someone else?"

"I don't have anyone else."

"Maybe get a roommate?"

"Oh, no. No way." He shook his head as he opened the passenger door for her.

"You are a stubborn man."

He shut the door and went around the car to the driver's side. Looking at Kat as he slid into the seat, he thought, *It had actually been really nice having Kat stay at my house when I was recovering. Not nearly as weird as I thought it was going to be.*

"What?" Kat, having finished buckling her seat belt, sat staring at him staring at her.

Dean smiled wanly. "Nothing. Just got lost for a second."

Kat frowned. "You've been doing that a lot today."

The keys rattled as he put the car key in the ignition but didn't start the engine. He took Kat's hand and leaned back against the headrest, closing his eyes. She'd already been his caretaker once. He didn't know what he wanted, exactly, but not that. He'd just have to get over this on his own, get his head in a good place to figure out what the future held for him and Kat. He squeezed her hand and looked at her. Gazing into the depths of her dark brown eyes, he couldn't see a future for him without her in it. "I'm fine, Kat." He smiled and laughed a little. "Or, at least I will be."

She rested her other hand against his cheek and leaned closer, her gaze boring into his. "I hope so."

With only a fleeting thought about what his breath might smell like after eating garlic bread with his salad, Dean tangled his fingers through the loose hair at the back of her head and pulled her in to a kiss. The fatigue, fear, and uncertainty faded to the background as warmth flooded through him. This was only their second kiss—and as his heart began to race and pleasant sensations tickled his every nerve ending, his fog-filled, endorphin-fueled mind wondered why he hadn't initiated more of this. For the first time in days, the tension in his shoulders relaxed. The idea that he should end the kiss, that it was verging on inappropriate out there in a public parking lot, pushed its way into his thoughts, but Kat shifted and pressed her lips harder against his—and the thought of ending it shot away like a rocket to the moon.

Dean finally pulled away with a sigh when headlights from someone pulling into the lot flooded his car. He rested his forehead on hers for several seconds, enjoying the hum of electricity coursing through him.

"I'd better get you home," he said, his voice huskier than normal.

During the short drive to her house, Dr. Graves thought about the science involved in a kiss. Back in his college days, to his great protest, a female biology professor had given him a special assignment to gather studies related to kissing and write up a comprehensive paper describing, in scientific terms of course, why kissing was good for you. Only in this moment did Dean wonder if the professor had been flirting with him.

He smiled over at Kat and his heart leapt. The oxytocin, dopamine, and serotonin released into his bloodstream from their kiss still circulated, giving him a sense of euphoria. The happy hormones had completely replaced the cortisol that had been steadily rising over the last several days, causing his stress and anxiety. The tension headache that had been a near constant companion disappeared as the lengthy kiss had dilated his blood vessels, thus lowering his blood pressure.

Kissing was indeed good for you. He silently thanked the flirtatious professor as he walked Kat up to her porch. "If it's okay with you"—he pulled her close as they reached the door—"I'd like to kiss you again."

Kat smiled and leaned into him, meeting his lips with hers as she tilted her head back.

Dean thought he just might actually get a good night's sleep tonight. He hummed *The Hills are Alive* as he walked back to his car.

SIX

The happy kissing hormones lasted most of the night. Dr. Graves' dreams started out pleasant—discombobulatingly pleasant—but ended once again in terror, sweat-soaked tangled sheets, and a much earlier wake-up time than he wanted.

The nightmare still played in his head as he pulled into the deserted parking lot at the morgue, drops of rain glowing in the dim light of the too few street lamps. Dr. Graves had been the first to arrive there many times throughout his years as Augusta's M.E., but this was the first time fear gripped him at the thought of walking from his car to the entrance. And entering the dark building. He didn't realize how tight his fingers were clenched around the steering wheel until the ache in his knuckles forced his mind to take notice.

He peeled his hands away and flexed his fingers to get the blood circulating again. Taking a deep breath, Dr. Graves tried to convince his body to abort the fight-or-flight adrenaline spike making his heart pound rapid-fire against his sternum. "This is ridiculous!" he said out loud.

With a forceful exhale, he flung his door open, shoved his keys in his pocket, and headed toward the back entrance, compelling himself to walk at a quick but steady pace even though the phantom screaming "Danger!" in his head begged him to run. He badged into the employee entrance, ignoring the tremor in his usually steady hand. The automatic overhead lights clicked on, illuminating the hallway leading to the elevators. Dr. Graves blew out the breath he'd been holding, checked to make sure the door had latched behind him, and hurried to the elevator.

He closed his eyes as it descended to the basement. Through gritted teeth, he forced himself to breathe slowly. The doors whooshed open, and he stepped out, the familiarity of his surroundings calming his frayed nerves. Using his badge to activate the sliding doors into the morgue, Dr. Graves was met with the familiar odors of disinfectant and formaldehyde.

The auto lights flicked on as he stepped into the autopsy suite. A manila envelope sat atop the stainless-steel autopsy table; there must have been a body delivered sometime during the night. He walked over and picked it up, his hand brushing against the cold metal. He froze, envelope raised just inches above where it had lain. His throat closed around a cry as he was transported back to the condemned jail; *a tremor washed over him, the areas of his body that had been pressed against the metal table as he lay there, unable to move, chilled. The straps holding him down tightened about his chest, arms, legs...*

His vision faded around the edges. He needed oxygen, but he forgot how to breathe. *Carter Ridge's voice echoed inside his head,* "It's time to get started..."

The phone on the wall behind him rang. He dropped the envelope and gasped in a breath of air, spinning around, eyes darting to the phone, the door, the hallway, the wall of refrigerated drawers. Dr. Graves blinked, his blurred vision coming back into focus as the flashback faded. He looked at the flashing light on the phone, noting it was his office line. It would have to go to voicemail, he was in no shape to answer it right now.

After catching his breath, he stomped to his office, flipped on the lights, and slammed the door shut. The terror that had taken him hostage a few moments ago turned to anger. He pulled at his hair with both hands, seething, chest heaving as he tried to gain control of his thoughts. His anger wasn't even directed toward the killer whose actions had turned his life upside down; it was directed inwardly. He, Dr. Dean Graves, should have been able to analyze, to reason, to use logic to control this...whatever was going on.

He slammed his fist into the wall next to the door, his hand disappearing through the drywall up past his wrist. Pain flared in the small bones that ran along the pinky side of his hand. Dean pulled his fist out and examined it. Looking at the hole in the wall, he was tempted to do it again—the sharp pain had cleared his head.

He could not allow this to keep happening. He trudged to his desk and fell into his chair, wincing as he dropped his head into his hands for several minutes. How could his emotions fluctuate so drastically in less than twelve hours? He tried to resurrect the pure joy and comfort he'd experienced while kissing Kat, and for several hours afterward.

Kat. Crap! What time is it? Dean looked at his watch and relaxed his shoulders a bit. She wouldn't be there for another hour. He could get himself together by then. Coffee first. He went to the small breakroom and started a pot brewing—it wasn't as good as their favorite coffee shop, but it would get the job done.

While the coffee brewed, he retrieved the manila envelope he'd dropped in the morgue and took it back to his desk, noticing the blinking voicemail light on his phone as he set it down. He picked up the phone and punched in his PIN#, then examined his swelling hand while he listened to the message.

"Dean, this is Liz. I didn't think you'd be in this early, but I just wanted to give you a call real quick while I had a minute. The PCR from the autopsy you helped with came back. Give me a call when you get in."

I should get some ice on this, Dr. Graves thought as he dialed Dr. Allen's office number. She picked up on the second ring. "Dr. Allen," she sounded distracted.

"Hi, Liz. Dr. Graves here, returning your call."

"Oh, Dean, hi. So, the PCR from that first patient came back positive for *Legionella pneumophila,* as we suspected, but the weird thing is that the sample contained three different serogroups—one, five, and ten."

"That's...very unusual. Three different serogroups?"

"That isn't all. The pathologist also isolated a fourth serogroup, but he isn't sure what it is. He said it's definitely *Legionella* and has characteristics most resembling *L. dumofii*, but it differs by two alleles."

"So basically, if I'm remembering my pathophysiology and microbiology correctly, it's highly unlikely that this is something that occurred naturally."

"Exactly," Liz agreed. "That's what the pathologist said."

"So we're looking at a possible bioterrorist?"

"Well, no one wants to come right out and say that, but between you and me, I don't see what else it could be."

Dr. Graves tightened his grip on the phone and winced at the pain in his hand. "Great. Any other news?"

"Unfortunately there have been two more deaths, a twenty-six-year-old male and a nineteen-year-old female. I'll be doing their autopsies today."

"Anything on the contact tracing?"

"No connections between patients yet. What's happening in Augusta? I know you have a few cases, anything new?"

He wedged the phone between his ear and shoulder and opened the envelope he'd found on the autopsy table. A sticky-note attached to the front of an autopsy request form had "*Locker 5-A*" written on it. Dr. Graves peeled the note off and glanced at the request. "Looks like we have our first death, came in overnight."

They discussed how to proceed and which samples to send to the state lab before wishing each other luck and hanging up.

Dr. Graves flipped through the deceased's medical chart then stood, remembering the coffee he'd brewed before calling Dr. Allen. After only two steps toward the breakroom he heard the sliding doors open. He turned around, instant warmth flooding his chest at the sight of Kat walking toward him, hair pulled up into a tight ponytail, looking down as she clipped her ID badge to her shirt.

"Kat." The relief in his voice surprised him.

She looked up and smiled. "Dean...umm...Dr. Graves, I mean."

Her reversion to using his formal title reminded him where they were, and he stopped just short of embracing her. "I'm so happy you're here."

Her brow wrinkled as she studied him. "How long have you been here? Is everything okay?"

"Yes. Everything's fine. I woke up early, so I just came in." He didn't want to worry her more than he already had. Besides, they had an autopsy to perform. "I'm going to have a cup of coffee then we need to get started, our first *Legionella* victim came in last night."

"Oh. Shoot." She followed him down the hall. "Let me put my stuff away and I'll go get everything ready." She turned into her office. "Wait. *Victim?*" She poked her head back out the door.

Dr. Graves nodded. "Looks like this isn't just a naturally occurring phenomenon. I'll explain while we work."

With a frown and a nod, Kat's head disappeared through the doorway. The urge to follow her was so strong, Dr. Graves had to keep reminding himself they were at work. He poured two cups of coffee and took one in to Kat, setting it on her desk in front of her.

"Thank—" She grabbed his hand as he realized his mistake and tried to jerk it back before she got a good look. "What did you do to your hand?" She turned it to where she could examine the swelling, a mean purple bruise forming.

He pulled it from her loose grip and grimaced. He couldn't lie to her, but he was mortified to admit that he'd lost control like a rampaging baboon. His neck and face heated up, and he looked down, unable to meet her eyes. "I uhh, I—" Damnit! He was ashamed to admit he'd lost control. Didn't want to tell her about the flashback. The latest nightmare... A rush of emotions took him by surprise and it was all he could do to swallow it down. He had always been so stoic, some people even called him unfeeling, hardhearted—well, just the one girl he'd dated in college—but the last few days his moods had been all over the place, like a pregnant woman's. Or a teenager.

Kat reached across her desk and touched his face. "Dean."

He sighed and looked up at her through a couple of wayward curls falling into his eyes. It was time to get a haircut again. He shrugged and tried to smile. "I had a bad morning...and I...I took it out on the wall in my office."

She huffed. "And your hand. I bet it's broken, a boxer's fracture. Are you going to be able to do the autopsy?"

Wondering how she knew about boxer's fractures, he answered, "I'll be fine. It'll be a little tender, but I deserve a little pain for letting myself lose control like that."

"Oh, Dean, you're the last person on Earth who deserves pain." The sincerity and compassion in her voice caused another rogue wave of emotions to crash into his chest.

He cleared his throat and whispered somewhat hoarsely, "Well, we uhh, we should get to work."

—◡—

WHILE KAT FINISHED LABELING and sending specimens, and cleaning and autoclaving instruments, Dr. Graves sat at his desk, an icepack resting on his hand, checking his inbox. The pathology report and some of the lab results were back on the young man with the deodorant spray problem.

He typed the results into his report then printed it out and signed it. Kat stepped into his office holding a biohazard bag. "Here are the specimens that need to go to the state lab. The courier will be here before five to pick it up. Does it need to be refrigerated or anything?"

"Yes, frozen actually, I'm glad you asked." He looked up at her and smiled. She really was one in a million. "I'll have this autopsy report on the nineteen-year-old from last week ready to send to the detectives here in a minute."

"You got his results back already? What did they show?"

"Yeah, well, I got the important results back. It was just as I thought, the butane and propane were both at 0.35 mg per liter—0.1 mg per liter can be fatal."

"But you don't think he was huffing it?"

"No, this was caused by absorption through his skin and by

passively breathing in the fumes. It built up over time, after months of overusing body spray." He shook his head. "So unfortunate."

Kat glanced at the hole in his wall as she left to put the specimens in the lab freezer. She sighed. "What are you going to do about your hand?"

"I texted my orthopedic doctor. I'm going to head over there in a few minutes so he can take an x-ray." Dean ran his uninjured hand through his hair. "It's going to be humiliating."

SEVEN

The soft wrap the ortho doctor had placed on Dr. Graves' fractured hand yesterday—his fourth and fifth fingers buddy-taped together—was awkward, especially while he attempted to make dinner for himself and Kat. Maybe he shouldn't have tried a new recipe. His hand throbbed, and he growled as he lost his grip on the fork while attempting to shred the rotisserie chicken. It clanged to the tile, and he bent to pick it up just as Kat knocked lightly then opened the front door and let herself in.

"Do you need some help, Muhammad Ali?" The smirk on her face was adorable.

"Ha ha." He threw the fork in the sink and pulled another one from the drawer. "I thought this would be easier than cooking chicken from scratch... I was wrong."

Kat set her phone and keys down on the counter and nudged him out of the way with her hip, holding her hand out to him. "Here, let me do this. Are you trying to shred it?" She glanced at the pitiful little pile of shredded chicken in the bowl next to the carcass and raised an eyebrow at him.

Handing over the fork with a sigh, he said, "Yes, that is what I was attempting."

While she worked the chicken over like a pro, he gathered the other ingredients for the chicken ranch taco recipe he'd pulled off an "easy recipes" website. Not so easy with a broken hand, it seemed. In less than five minutes, Kat handed him the bowl full of meat and said, "What else do you need help with?"

"I'm sorry, Kat. I'm supposed to be fixing dinner for you."

"Oh, I'll be sure to hold it against you until you make it up to me." She grinned and winked at him.

Dean mixed the spices and meat together then heated it in the microwave while Kat cut up a tomato and some lettuce. Luckily, he'd thought to buy already shredded cheese—trying to use a cheese grater would have been disastrous.

All in all, the tacos turned out to be pretty good as they ate on his patio, enjoying the mild early-summer weather.

Kat carried the empty plates inside. Winston, the neighbor's Golden Retriever, loped over to Dean and dropped a slobbery tennis ball at his feet, looking up at him expectantly. "You haven't been over to see me in over a week and you just expect me to play fetch with you?" Dean scratched the dog behind the ears before pulling a gardening glove onto his left hand to avoid the dog slobber. "Not sure how well this is going to work throwing with my left hand, but I'll give it a try."

While Winston ran after the ball, Kat returned and sat in the Adirondack chair next to Dean. "You ready to tell me about why you had such a bad morning and went all Rocky Balboa on the office wall?"

Winston's return gave him a moment to gather his thoughts while he picked up the ball and threw it lamely with his non-dominant hand. He was definitely not ambidextrous. "I had another nightmare, early this morning, so I just decided to go into work early." Did he want to tell her the next part?

She waited in silence. She knew there was more to it, and he knew he needed to talk to someone about it—and Kat was his someone.

Dean wiped the sweat from his brow, his pulse sped up and he gritted his teeth at the unpleasant fluttering in his chest. He looked down at his lap. "I had a flashback at work this morning, before you got there." He turned to meet her gaze. He forced the next words out around a lump in his throat. "I think I have PTSD."

Her steady gaze never wavered. She laid her hand on his arm and squeezed. "I don't know how you could *not* have PTSD after what you went through, Dean."

The clicking of Winston's claws on the patio caused him to break eye contact with Kat. The blasted intelligent furry creature took one look at Dean, dropped the ball, whined, and laid his head on Dean's lap, looking up at him with what could only be described as the clichéd "puppy-dog eyes." Dean shook the glove off his left hand and buried his fingers in the thick fur around the dog's neck. The tenseness in his shoulders instantly relaxed, and he was able to swallow the lump in his throat. "I know this sounds...*arrogant* maybe? But I always thought of psychology as a pseudo-science, like the diagnoses didn't really count because there isn't any hard evidence for them. Nothing you can see through a microscope or run a blood test for."

"I can see you thinking that. But, Dean, not everything in life can be examined through the lens of a microscope. Not everything is as cut and dry as the number of white blood cells, or a glucose level. The human brain is much more complex than that."

He leaned his head back and closed his eyes, still scratching Winston's neck. "I know. It's hard for me to admit it, but I've always known that. I just thought I could use reason and data, evidence, *reality*, to whip my mind back into shape." He sat forward and turned his head to look at Kat. "But this morning, Kat, this morning... I could *feel* the cold table against my skin, the straps holding me down, tightening around me." His voice hitched. "I couldn't *breathe*, Kat. I... I heard his voice."

"Oh, Dean."

The dog whined, put his paws on Dean's lap, and lifted up to lick a tear from his cheek. Dean hadn't even realized he was crying. He wiped his face and gave Winston a gentle push. "Get down, boy."

Kat watched this exchange with a thoughtful look on her face. "Maybe you should see someone. A therapist."

He shook his head. "No. I don't see that working for me."

She rolled her eyes. "How about a group or something, like the one Sam runs in Captain America for the veterans?"

Dr. Graves smiled and reached for Winston's head again. "Only if Captain Steve Rogers attends the same group."

A small laugh bubbled to her lips before she turned serious again. "Dean, you can't just keep going on like this. You aren't getting enough sleep, you're barely eating. Your mood swings are giving me whiplash."

"Kat," his stomach twisted into a tight knot, "I'm so sorry. Please forgive me. I've been so wrapped up in what's going on in my own head that I didn't even stop to consider how my behavior is affecting you. Please," he cupped her cheek in his hand, "please forgive me."

She covered his hand with hers. "There's nothing to forgive. I just want to help you through this."

"You are helping. This helps, talking, being with you."

Nodding slowly, she said, "I'm going to ask you one more time: do you want me to stay with you for a few days?" She hurried to add, "I'll stay in the guest bedroom."

"No," he rushed to say before the fluttering in his stomach could convince him otherwise. The next time Kat stayed overnight, he didn't want it to be as a caretaker. Heat rushed to his face with that thought and he looked away, stuttering, "I...I mean...thank you, for offering. But I need to work this out on my own." That wasn't what he wanted to say. He needed her... "That's...that's not completely true." He sighed and tilted his head back, looking up at the sky. "I... need your help. I've been alone for so long, it's hard for me to admit that. Hell, it's hard for me to recognize how valuable your support is. But my nervous system recognizes it. My blood pressure normalizes. I breathe easier when you're around. My heart rate slows down," he grinned, "until you kiss me—but that's the good kind of tachycardia."

She laughed, shaking her head. "I feel like there's another 'but' in there somewhere."

Dean nodded. "I'm not sure how to word this... I don't want you to see me at my weakest ever again. I don't want you to have to take care of me again, babysit me. That's why I'm turning down your considerate offer to stay with me."

He fully expected her to argue with him, but she surprised him with her response. "Okay. I understand, and I won't ask again, but please remember that it's an open offer. If you ever change your mind, I'll be here as fast as I can."

He leaned in for a kiss, but was interrupted by his neighbor, Amy. "Winston! Leave Dr. Graves alone. Get over here!"

The dog grabbed his tennis ball and ran back to his own yard. "Sorry, Dr. Graves," Amy said.

"It's no problem. He's kind of growing on me." Dr. Graves waved as Amy and the dog went into their house.

As the sun set, Dean looked at his watch. "My mother would be very disappointed in me for keeping you so late on a weekday when we both have to work in the morning." He chuckled. "Come to think of it, she'd be disappointed that we are here alone, without a chaperone."

"Really? Was she super religious or old fashioned or something?"

"She was religious, but it wasn't that, really. She taught me to respect women, told me she'd beat me with a switch if I ever kissed a girl on the first date. 'Girls are more than just sex objects, Dean,' she'd say. 'A woman deserves a long courtship—and a wedding ring—before you just jump into bed with her.'" He glanced at Kat with a sheepish grin. "She really didn't need to worry, I didn't even date in high school."

"Not even prom?" Kat's eyes widened.

"Not even prom."

"What about in college?"

How had he allowed himself to get into this uncomfortable conversation? "I dated, a little. My roommates used to make fun of me for being a prude."

He could see realization strike Kat as her eyebrows rose. *Please don't ask what I think you're going to ask*, he begged silently, trying to think of some way to quickly change the subject.

"Wait, does that mean you've never..."

Too late. She asked. Shame wouldn't allow him to look her in the eye as he thought about how to answer. "I...have, actually...once." He rubbed his face. "I dated a girl, a woman, my last year of medical school. She was ready for...more...by our second date, but I explained to her that I thought we should get to know each other better first. I guess she lost patience with me after a couple of months though, because she conspired with my roommates to get me drunk, really drunk. I barely remember that night. Just bits and pieces. The hangover was bad, but the disgust I felt for myself was the worst. She came back the next night, thinking now that the ice had been broken, I'd be a more willing participant."

"You broke up with her, didn't you?" Kat stated it as a known fact, not a question.

Dean nodded. "I felt terrible. She just thought I was an eccentric weirdo and hooked up with one of my roommates soon after."

"Well, she basically date-raped you, so she's the one that should have felt terrible. Is that why you don't drink alcohol?"

"Partly, yes. But I also don't like not being in complete control of my actions."

"That does not surprise me a bit." She took his hand and waited for him to look at her. "This whole PTSD thing is sort of like that for you, isn't it? I mean, the not being in control part."

He breathed out a prolonged breath. The way she just skipped over the sexual encounter confession gave him some hope that it didn't bother her. "Yes. Being unable to regulate my thoughts and emotions is maddening."

"Well, Dean Graves, I'm sure your mother was very proud of you. You learned her lessons of respect well, and I, for one, am grateful to her for that." She stood and pulled on his hand until he stood up. She raised up on her toes and kissed him, a short but breathtaking mingling of their lips. "On that note, I'm going to head home. See you in the morning."

As he walked Kat to her car, he thought about his mom. She'd been gone for over a year now, and he really missed her. He hoped Kat was right about her being proud of him.

EIGHT

"Dean," Chief Tracey Billings stopped him in the parking lot Thursday morning, "you look terrible. Is everything okay?"

He tried to smile and wave off her concern. "I'm fine. Just didn't sleep well last night."

Tracey raised an eyebrow. "Looks like more than one night of poor sleep." She walked beside him toward the city building. "Are you seeing anyone, a therapist or someone, to help you process what happened to you?"

Not Tracey, too. They'd been friends for a long time and had had many serious conversations over the years, deep down he knew she was just showing concern, but the irritation that blossomed in his guts came bubbling out of his mouth before he could stop it. "I don't need to see anyone. I'm fine. People have trouble sleeping all the time, it doesn't mean they need to be committed to a mental health institution, for hell's sake!"

"Whoa," she held up her hands in a placating gesture, "ain't no one suggesting that, Dr. Graves."

Instant guilt smacked into him. "I'm sorry, Tracey. It was wrong for me to snap at you. I am fine, though."

"Are you trying to convince me or yourself of that?"

"Tracey, seriously, drop it."

They reached the door, and he held it open for her. She stopped and looked at him, a flicker of tenderness in her hardened face. "I've seen a lot of trauma reactions during my time in law enforcement, Dean, so you can't pull one over on me. I get that you don't want to talk about it right now, but if you change your mind, I'm here for you." She walked past him into the building.

He hung his head for a few seconds then followed her to the third-floor boardroom where they'd been asked to participate in a statewide teleconference to discuss the pneumonia deaths.

An overweight man wearing round glasses popped up on the screen. "Let's get started, we won't take up much of your time, I know y'all have a lot to do. I'm Dr. James and I work at the CDC here in Atlanta. What I'm about to say stays between us, we are very early on in the investigation into this disease, and the ideas I express here are merely speculation at this point. Some of you may have heard that we've isolated four different serogroups of *Legionella* from the samples that have come in so far. This is very unusual and unlikely to have occurred naturally. We may be looking at an act of bioterrorism, but we also may be just looking at a scientific phenomenon involving mutation.

"Our first priority has been to come up with a treatment plan for those affected with this highly fatal strain of pneumonia. Preliminary results from our specialty lab show a super potent bacteria that is extremely resistant to many antibiotics. Our recommendation for treatment consists of hitting the patient hard and fast with parenteral fluoroquinolones and macrolides, ideally within the first twenty-four hours of symptom onset—in other words, don't wait for lab results to come back, just assume we're dealing with what we're now calling *Legionella* Tetrad."

"Dr. James," one of the infectious disease doctors in Atlanta interrupted, "what specific fluoroquinolones and macrolides do you recommend at this point?"

"Good question. As you know, we haven't had time to conduct any studies, so this recommendation is based on past *Legionella* studies and on the sensitivity results that are slowly trickling in. It appears that the best treatment to date is a combination of levofloxacin, rifampin, and azithromycin at the highest recommended doses." Dr. James sighed. "But if any of you show good results with another combination, please share with the group. We'll send out a group email to y'all so we can all stay in touch."

The meeting went on for another hour, with very little new information being shared. Dr. Graves had to get up and pace in the small space at the back of the room in order to stay alert, while Chief Billings glanced at him at frequent intervals, trying to hide her concern behind a scowl.

—∧—

BY THE TIME he made it to the morgue parking lot, he decided he either needed a nap or an entire pot of coffee. He groaned a little when he saw the detectives' unmarked police cruiser parked illegally at the curb near the employee entrance. "What now?" he mumbled as he climbed out of his car.

Kat had already removed the young deceased man from the body bag and prepped the instrument table. Detectives Davis and Fitzpatrick were again accompanied by Detective Rodriguez. Dr. Graves nodded at them and smiled at Kat. "What did you bring us this time, detectives?" He looked at Rodriguez as he said this, hoping she would be the one to give the report again. She seemed much more professional than the two practical jokers he usually had to deal with.

Rodriguez nodded, her face solemn. "We have here a sixteen-year-old male, found down in a storage shed on his family's property. EMS was not able to revive him. His sixteen-year-old friend was also found unconscious and was transported to the ER in critical condition."

She walked over to the body and pointed to the right side of the boy's face. "The only visible marks upon a cursory inspection is what appears to be a blister and redness to his face—the side of his face that was touching the floor—and a bump with mild bruising to his forehead on that same side. The other boy had no visible marks and was found lying halfway out the door, convulsing and frothing at the mouth." She gestured to the clothing the deceased wore. "They both were wearing the same type of clothing—long pants tucked into high-top sneakers, long-sleeved shirts, thick work gloves, and goggles. Very strange for this time of year."

Examining the facial injury, Dr. Graves tilted his head. "What kind of surface was this boy found on?"

"The cement floor of the shed, sir."

He almost smiled—for as long as he'd worked with Detectives Davis and Fitzpatrick, they'd never called him "sir." He looked up at Detective Rodriguez. "Were there any chemicals on the floor?"

"None that were apparent."

"Any strong odors?"

She shook her head. "No, sir."

Dr. Graves looked back at the young boy laying on the cold table and thought for a moment. "Any drug paraphernalia found?"

"No, sir."

"When were the deceased and his friend last seen alive and well?"

"An hour or less before 9-1-1 was called."

"Hmmm." He rubbed his hands through his hair. "Okay. Please have the crime scene photographer send me the photos right away." He looked at the three detectives. "And check these boys' social media posts; see if either of them posted anything...unusual recently."

"Yeah, okay," Fitzpatrick said. "We'll get someone on that—"

"*Today*," Dr. Graves said. "I'm sort of at a loss here and I need some external content to know what to look for." He dismissed them with, "I'll be expecting a call from you within the hour, detectives."

Detective Rodriguez handed him the paperwork with a sharp nod. "Yes, sir. Consider it done."

"Thank you, Detective Rodriguez," he smiled. "I hope these two are learning something from you."

"Hey!" Davis protested. "*We* are teaching *her*. She's a greenie."

Dr. Graves raised an eyebrow at him. "That doesn't mean you can't learn from her, Davis. Now go do what I asked, I need to get started here."

Rodriguez's laughter and Davis and Fitzpatrick's mumbling followed the detectives out the door.

Dean touched Kat's arm. "I'm going to grab a cup of coffee before getting started. I'll be right back."

Kat nodded, already in full-on work mode. "Is it okay if I start cutting off his clothes?"

"Yes. Thank you."

He limited himself to a half cup of coffee before returning. As Dr. Graves donned a surgical gown, mask, and goggles, Kat took x-rays.

At a frustrated growl from him, Kat looked up from positioning the x-ray arm and raised her eyebrows. "Everything okay?"

"I can't get a glove over this stupid splint. I'm taking it off."

As he ripped the Velcro straps away and pulled the soft splint off, Kat put a hand on her lead-lined aproned hip and said, "Are you sure that's a good idea?"

"Probably not." He shrugged. "But I'm doing it, anyway."

Kat shook her head and returned her attention to the x-ray machine.

After awkwardly and somewhat painfully pulling new gloves on, Dr. Graves examined the red, blistered skin on the boy's face and grabbed a pick-up forceps and a scalpel from the table. "I'm going to take some small samples of this skin, here. Will you prepare a slide, please? I'd like to take a look at it under the microscope. And I'll send a sample to pathology—"

Before he could request a formalin specimen container, Kat had one open, holding it out to him in one hand while holding a microscope slide in the other. He smiled beneath his mask. "You're the best, Kat."

She shrugged and winked. "I know."

He stopped himself from chuckling because it would be disrespectful while working on the deceased, but his heart grew lighter. He placed the small skin samples on the slide and into the container.

"That reminds me of what my skin looked like when I had cryotherapy on a mole." Kat labeled the specimen and set it aside.

"It does, doesn't it?" Dr. Graves positioned the overhead light to see it better. "It's definitely not a thermal burn. Maybe chemical..." He examined the area again. "I need to see those photos. From the detectives' report, I don't see what could have caused this."

The rest of the autopsy was unremarkable. The lungs showed moderate congestion, and the brain showed some mild edema and congestion. Everything else seemed to be in normal condition.

As they cleaned the body and prepared to place it back in the body bag, Kat asked, "So, any thoughts on what killed this boy?"

Dr. Graves frowned and shook his head. "I have no idea. I'm hoping the information I asked the detectives to get will give me some more clues."

Kat zipped up the bag. "Why don't you go see if they've sent you anything while I clean up and get the blood and tissue samples ready to go."

"All right." He pulled his surgical gown off, pulling the sleeves inside out and removing the gloves along with it, balled it up and stuffed it in the large trash receptacle labeled "biohazard," washed his hands, then took the mask and goggles off. He headed straight for the break room and poured another cup of sub-par coffee, inhaling its scent as he walked back to his office.

Dr. Graves sat at his desk and took a sip from the "Mischief Managed" mug Chief Billings had given him a few years ago. He set it down and signed in to his computer. As the little blue circle spun on the screen, he flexed his aching hand then rubbed his temples. He should probably drink some water—even though his dad had always said "coffee's mostly water," Dr. Graves knew better. One click on his email icon and he forgot all about hydrating. He'd received two emails from Isabella Rodriguez. As he clicked on the first one labeled "photos," he mumbled, "I wonder if I can trade Fitzpatrick for her."

He pulled up the photos and zoomed in on the first one. He took notes on a yellow legal pad as he scanned the picture.

Small wet mark on cement near mouth – frothing like friend? This was circled with chalk and labeled on the photo since the victim had been moved during the resuscitation attempt and wasn't positioned the same in the photo as when he'd been found.

A wide shot of the interior of the shed caught his eye, and he clicked on it.

Common items found in shed.

Gas can – but no odor per LE or on deceased.

Weed killer spray on shelf – doesn't appear to have been moved/used.

Two large...pillow cases? Or cloth bags of some sort. Laying on floor near deceased.

Two big metal shovels – also laying on floor.

"Wait," Dr. Graves whispered, "what's this?" He zoomed in on a large, black metal tank. A faded, green, diamond-shaped label near the top read "NON-FLAMMABLE GAS 2." What probably used to be a white label to the side was too worn to read, curling up at the edges. There was a black hose attached to the regulator. Dr. Graves searched around the tank, clicking on other photos, to see if there was any welding equipment or other clues as to its use. None.

Shaking his head in frustration, Dr. Graves opened the second email containing screen shots of the boys' social media posts. He scrolled through the screen shots and thought, with a pit of sadness forming in his gut, *These boys are just typical teenagers. What happened to them?* He stopped on a post by the deceased from two weeks earlier that said, "Watched one of my dad's favorite movies from back in the day called Real Genius. It was LIT! Me and Jeff gonna try something from the movie. I'll post a video if it works!"

Dr. Graves shot up, nearly knocking his chair over. His level of alertness hit an all-time high—well, not all-time, but a recent high at least.

"I'm starving, wanna—" Kat stopped in his doorway and raised her eyebrows. "What?"

"I think I figured it out. I need to call Tracey." He grabbed the phone and hit the button programmed with the Chief of Police's office number.

She picked up on the second ring. "Chief Billings."

"Tracey, Dr. Graves here. I think I might know what happened to our DOA today, but I need some information from the scene for confirmation."

"Let me grab Davis, he's just standing around, anyway."

He was hoping for Rodriguez, but would have to settle.

"I'm gonna put you on speaker phone, Dean," Tracey said.

"Detective," Dr. Graves began, "that big tank in the shed, the black one, did it happen to contain carbon dioxide? CO_2?"

"Possibly. It doesn't belong to the parents, they've never seen it before today. We tracked it back to the high school the dead kid went —Ouch!" Davis's voice lowered. "Sorry, boss. I mean *the deceased's* high school. Rodriguez is working on contacting the welding teacher."

Okay. He'd have to go with his gut for now. "What are the dimensions of that shed? And were there any open windows or doors other than the one the other young man was found by?"

"The shed is ten-by-ten, and no open windows or doors other than that one. And it was stinkin' *hot* in there."

Dr. Graves tapped his fingers on his desk. "Okay... I think that's all for now. Let me know as soon as you find out anything about the contents of that tank." He hung up and looked at Kat who stood in front of his desk holding his hand splint out to him.

"Well? What did you figure out?" she asked.

He shook his head. "I can't believe this is what I'm thinking, but," he scrunched his forehead, "have you ever seen a movie from the eighties called *Real Genius*?" He took the splint from her and put it back on, admitting to himself that it really did help with the pain.

"Is that the one with a really young Val Kilmer?"

"Yes, that's the one."

"I've seen it. It was a long time ago—We watched it on VHS tape. My friend, Suzy, and I used to watch at least one of her parents' old videos almost every Saturday." She cocked her head. "What does that have to do with this case?"

"Do you remember the scene, I think it was right at the beginning, with the ice rink in the dorm?"

"Yes," she drew the word out and narrowed her eyes. "I loved that part."

"Well, these two unfortunate boys watched the movie a couple of weeks ago, and the deceased posted that they were going to 'try something' from the movie. I think that's the scene he was referencing."

"But...that was just fictional, right? I mean, like the popcorn thing at the end, I just figured it was poetic license for the script."

Dr. Graves shrugged. "To a teenager that has the internet at his fingertips, I'm sure he truly thought he knew how it was done."

"How?" Kat asked with a shake of her head.

"In the movie, the ice basically disappeared in a cloud of gas. It didn't turn into water like normal ice. What's the first substance that comes to mind that would react like that?" he answered her question with a question.

"Dry ice, I guess...which I don't even know how it's made, so my next question might be dumb, but how would that have killed him?"

"You never ask dumb questions, Kat, and in this instance that's the exact question you should be asking.

"It's actually very simple to make dry ice, you just need carbon dioxide and something to put it in that will catch the solid pieces as they form and let the vapor escape through the material." He opened the right photo and turned his computer screen to face her. "Like pillow cases or the like."

Her eyes widened as she looked from him to the screen and back again.

Dean continued. "I'm betting that big black tank contains one-hundred-percent CO_2 in gas form." Anticipating her next question he said, "It's used for certain welding techniques, and the boys may have gotten it from a local high school."

He took a sip of his coffee, wishing it was from the coffee shop down the street instead of from the break room. "My guess is that they were spraying the gas into the pillow cases, or whatever those are, then dumping the chunks of ice onto the floor and trying to mold or smash them together with the shovels to create a smooth surface—which probably wasn't working the way they hoped. As dry ice 'melts', or in reality, vaporizes back into its gas form, it pushes the oxygen out of the room, thus causing suffocation. That wouldn't be much of a problem in a well-ventilated area, but the windows were closed, and I'm assuming they had the door closed until the friend realized they were in trouble and opened it before succumbing to the lack of oxygen."

Nodding, Kat said, "That theory would explain the burn-not-burn on the deceased's face too. He must have passed out and landed on a piece of the dry ice, cryo-freezing his skin."

"Yes! I wasn't even thinking about that, but yes, that makes perfect sense." Dr. Graves' stomach growled, and he grinned. "What was that you were saying about being hungry?"

"Finish up and let's go get dinner." Kat stood and smiled at him before going to her own office.

He typed a quick email to Rodriguez: *Detective, please check the deceased's search history on his devices. I'm specifically looking for any searches on how to make dry ice. Thank you sincerely, Dr. Dean Graves.*

After turning his computer and monitor off, Dr. Graves ran his hand through his hair, unsuccessfully trying to tame the loose curls, and walked to Kat's office, feeling much lighter than when the day had started.

NINE

"Five new cases of the new *Legionella* strain the CDC is calling *Legionella* Tetrad were hospitalized in Atlanta over the weekend..."

Dr. Graves changed the radio station; he wasn't in the mood to listen to the media's spin on what was now being officially characterized as an epidemic. He jabbed at a button to turn the radio off when an obnoxious used car dealership commercial came on. "Why they feel the need to record their ads using bad Scottish accents is something I'll never understand." His mood turned sour, and he needed something to prevent it from getting worse.

"Maybe the head of the marketing team had an unnatural obsession with Shrek growing up." Kat turned to face him from the passenger seat of his car and said, "Ogres are like onions," with a terrible accent that might have resembled Scottish to a man raised by wolves in the deepest recesses of a vast, unexplored forest.

Dean laughed so hard he nearly had to pull over. Once he regained some semblance of control he said, "That had to be the worst attempt at a Scottish accent I've ever heard. And yet, it was incredibly adorable." Sour mood banished...for now.

"Let's hear yours," she countered.

Dean shook his head. "Oh, no. I do a much better Donkey impression."

"Okay, I'm listening." Kat's grin was full of mischief.

He couldn't believe he was doing this. "...and in the morning, I'm makin' waffles!"

Kat laughed. "That was pretty good. Eddie Murphy would be proud."

Smiling, Dean pulled into his parking spot at the morgue.

"Thanks for the ride," Kat said. "My car should be ready by the time we get off work today."

"You're welcome. It was and is my pleasure." He touched her face and smiled. Maybe this day wouldn't be so bad after all.

They walked to the employee entrance, and Kat asked, "Do you have any new thoughts about the pneumonia cases?"

"I have a lot of thoughts, too many really, they just keep spinning around in my head. Liz and I were messaging back and forth all weekend after she got news of the five new cases. They're all from the same apartment building that just opened up. They all just moved in last week. Different apartments, no real contact between them." He scanned his ID badge and held the door open for her.

"Same building but different apartments?" She furrowed her brow. "No wonder your head's spinning. I can't wrap my mind around that."

"I know. They're testing the water there, and they shut the building down, but that's about all they can think of to do right now."

"So, do I have this right?" They entered the elevator and Kat pushed the button to the basement. "Same building, different apartments—but they couldn't have all been living alone, could they? Yet no one else in the same apartment with one of the patients is sick?"

"You've got it right. I know there's something there, something to that, but I can't figure it out. It just doesn't make sense."

As if she could sense his building frustration, Kat changed the subject as they entered the morgue. "How's your hand? Have you been resting it? Letting it heal?"

"It feels much better than last week. And yes, I rested it all weekend while you were stranded at your brother's with a broken-down car. I didn't even give in to the urge to paint."

"Good. How have you been sleeping? Any more nightmares...or anything?"

He assumed that by "or anything" she meant flashbacks. They stopped at his office door and he rubbed his eyes, holding in a sigh. He just wanted this to be over with. He wanted to feel normal again. "I got some sleep. Had a couple of nightmares. I'm fine." He faked a smile and touched her chin. "I'm okay. But I do have a video meeting to attend in a few minutes, so I'd better go get my computer up and running."

She pursed her lips, probably trying to decide if it was worth it to call him on his vagueness. To his relief she just nodded and said, "Okay. I'll bring you some coffee when it's ready."

Dean watched her walk the few steps down the hall and turn into the break room before letting out the sigh he'd been holding in. He went into his office and clicked the computer and monitor on then sat, laying his head on his desk. What he'd failed to divulge to Kat was that he'd had another flashback. In his own home. *In his own home!* He couldn't even safely flip through channels on the TV at three a.m. without being drug back into the inferno that was the hell of Carter Ridge.

The computer beeped, alerting him that he had unread messages. He raised his head and ran his hands through his hair. He signed into the web meeting and nodded his thanks to Kat when she set his mug of steaming coffee on the desk.

The only new information he learned from the meeting was that the cocktail of recommended antibiotics didn't seem to be making much of a difference. At least half of the patients being treated with the heavy-duty medications weren't responding, and there had been two more deaths. Not good odds.

He jumped when his desk phone rang even though it was set on the quietest setting. Dr. Graves scowled as he picked up the receiver. "Dr. Graves."

"Dean, this is Tracey. I just wanted to follow up with you on the sixteen-year-old. The tank did belong to the metal shop at the high school, and it did contain 100% CO_2. The boys must have lifted it Wednesday night after they told the teacher they'd lock up for him. Our IT guys went through both boys' phones and the deceased's laptop and they both had searches for 'how to make dry ice' on their devices." She paused. "Wanna tell me how you knew that and what the hell happened to these boys?"

Dr. Graves explained his theory, now a mostly proven theory, about the boys trying to recreate a scene from an '80s movie.

"Oh, yeah," Tracey said. "I remember that movie and that scene. Val Kilmer was hot back then."

"All geniuses are 'hot', Tracey," he quipped. "How's the friend doing?"

Her voice perked up a little. "It looks like he'll make it. They're going to wean him off the induced coma meds now that the swelling in his brain has gone down. We might be able to confirm your theory with him as soon as tomorrow if that goes well."

A weight lifted from Dean's chest. "That's great. Finally some good news."

-\/-

"Is it okay if I come over in about an hour?" Kat asked as Dean dropped her off to get her car from the shop. "I have something for you I brought back from my brother's. I'll bring pizza."

"Yes, that's—"

"Kay! See you soon." She shut the door and waved to him before going in to get her keys—and probably pay a huge bill.

Dean narrowed his eyes as he watched her walk away. "What is she up to?"

When he got home, he decided to sit out on the back porch even though it was sweltering hot and humid. He needed to soak in some of the sun's rays. Plus, he didn't really want to sit in his favorite chair in the living room—well, it used to be his favorite chair until he'd had a flashback while sitting in it.

He eased back into the Adirondack chair and tilted his head back against the house, closing his eyes. He was so tired.

Carter Ridge's face loomed over him, and Dean's heart vaulted against his ribs, looking for a way out. Dean's breaths came in short, quick bursts, not even coming close to bringing in enough oxygen or blowing out enough CO_2.

Something wet touched his hand, and a gentle whine made the face dissipate into the atmosphere. Dr. Graves looked down where the wet and the whine had come from. A sleek, chocolate-colored dog just slightly bigger than Winston sat at his feet.

Dean looked around the porch and his yard for the owner, then back at the dog. "Where did you come from?" He held his hand out for the dog to sniff...and it laid its head in his lap, looking up at him with beautiful golden eyes. He looked around again as he stroked the animal's head. "Wherever you came from, you got here just in time." Dean shivered as the vision in his dream crept into his thoughts.

The dog whined and licked his hand.

"Looks like you two have hit it off," Kat said from the doorway behind him.

"Kat! Is this...is this your dog?" He knew she didn't have a dog, at least she hadn't had one just a few days ago.

"Nope." She sat in the chair next to him and reached for his splinted hand. "She's yours."

"What?" He looked from her to the dog and back. "I can't, I mean, I don't have time to train a dog."

"No worries, she's already trained."

"But...what will I do with her while I'm at work?"

"She's crate trained, so she can stay in your house in a crate while you're at work. Or, I already talked to Amy, next door. She said she'd be happy to take care of her during the day. She and Winston can hang out." Kat patted his hand. "She's also a trained support animal, so you might be able to talk the higher-ups into letting you bring her to work with you if you want."

"Oh, no. Labs shed too much to take her there." He looked back at the dog. "She is a Lab, right?"

"Yes. A pure-bred."

"Kat," his voice hitched, and he swallowed, "she must have cost you a fortune. I...I can't accept—"

Shaking her head, Kat interrupted. "She didn't cost me anything. My oldest brother breeds and trains them, and he owes me big time for all the free babysitting I did for him and his wife as a teenager." She stood. "The pizza's in the house, and I have some things in my car I'll need your help to bring in."

He cleared his throat, staring down at the dog and fighting back tears as strong emotions warred inside him. "Be there in a sec."

Kat squeezed his shoulder and went back inside, gently closing the screen door behind her.

Had Kat known his childhood dog was a chocolate Lab? Cocoa. He sighed and rubbed the dog's head. Cocoa had been so comforting to him when his dad had died in a work accident when he was twelve. She'd put up with his angry outbursts, his quiet tears, and his months of grief. Losing Cocoa when he was sixteen tore him up all over again. A tear dripped down the bridge of his nose, hanging on the tip for a few seconds before splashing onto his arm. He swore he'd never have another dog. And yet here he sat, all emotional as the past collided with the present in his mind.

Wiping his face, Dean stood. "Well, we'd better go help Kat." The dog followed right at his heels as he walked through the house— the scent of pepperoni and pizza sauce made his stomach growl—and out the front door, meeting Kat at her car.

A million questions converged in his mind as she looked up at him. He pushed them all aside at the worry he saw in her eyes. As she chewed on her bottom lip, he realized she was probably wondering if she'd done the right thing, if he was mad at her. He pulled her to him in a tight embrace, no words passed between them as they stood in his driveway, in full view of his neighbors, holding each other.

How long in minutes they stood that way, Dean had no idea, he just knew it was long enough for Kat's warmth to flood him. Long enough to ease the tension that had been building in his muscles for days. Long enough for the dog at his side to decide it had been long enough. It nudged Dean's hip with a whine, then tried to squeeze between them.

Kat laughed and pulled away. "Hermione! Are you jealous already?"

The dog wagged her tail and *woofed*.

"Hermione?" Dean smiled.

"I thought you'd like that. My brother is also a big Harry Potter nerd. He has a gray tabby cat named Minerva."

Dean laughed. "I think your brother and I will get along just fine."

"I'm sure of it."

"How old is Hermione?" he asked as he lifted a fifty-pound bag of dogfood out of Kat's trunk.

"Ten months." Kat grunted as she struggled to get a large, folded up wire kennel out of her back seat.

"And what possessed you to get me a dog?"

She frowned slightly, concern darkening her eyes a touch. "You refuse to let a human help you, so I got you the next best thing. Well, actually, as loyal as dogs are it was probably the first best thing, with humans taking a distant second...or third."

"Well..." he looked down and mumbled, "thank you." He looked up again with a fake scowl. "But you're going to help with poop pick-up duty."

Kat smiled. "It's a deal."

They finally sat down to eat after carrying a large number of dog items into Dean's house. He looked at the pile as he chewed a bite of lukewarm pizza. "How did you fit all of that into your car?"

"Tetris champion of 2016," she quipped. "But, yeah, it was a tight squeeze."

After dinner Dean and Kat figured out where to put everything, Kat insisting that the dog bed go in Dean's bedroom, right next to his bed. "Dean, the main reason I got her for you is so she can help with your...sleeping issues. She has to be where you sleep to be able to do that."

He scowled, mostly just for show because he really wasn't feeling it. In fact, he felt better than he had in weeks. "Fine. But she'd better not try to get up on my bed."

—√—

Around midnight, Dean awoke to a sudden bounce of the mattress, pressure on his chest, and a dog tongue licking his face—just moments after a familiar serial killer appeared in his dream. Hermione had rescued him before his heart rate had even had a chance to hit peak fight-or-flight performance. He wiped the saliva off his face and pushed the dog off his chest with a, "Good girl, now get off me so I can breathe."

He laid there with Hermione sprawled out next to him, her chin resting on his chest, and his heart rate normalized within less than a minute. Dean knew he should make the dog get off his bed, but...well, his Cocoa had slept with him every night for eleven years, he guessed Hermione could too.

For the first time in weeks, he woke up to his alarm blaring instead of in cold sweats from a nightmare. Sometime during the night Hermione had returned to the floor but was now up on his bed again, wiggling and whining. "Okay, okay. Let me put a shirt and shoes on and I'll take you out to do your business."

Dean smiled. It was the first good night's sleep he'd gotten in a long time, and the first time, he realized, he felt hope return.

TEN

The line at the coffee shop was long, but Dean didn't mind. The aroma of fresh ground coffee made up for it. He smiled as he recalled how quickly Hermione and Winston had taken to each other. He'd have to get something for Amy for volunteering for dog-sitting duty.

Kat had just reached her office door when Dr. Graves entered the hallway, holding two hot cups of coffee. She turned toward him and smiled, walking to him and taking one of the cups from him. She opened the lid and inhaled as the steam escaped. "Oh, thank you! I almost forgot how much better coffee smells when it doesn't come from a can and isn't brewed in an antique coffeemaker."

Dr. Graves laughed as Kat took a sip. "Agreed. Why have we been brewing our own, anyway?"

"Good question. To save time, maybe?" She closed her eyes and held the cup below her nose, smelling the rich aroma again. "But it isn't worth it."

The ringing phone in his office interrupted their banter as they went their separate ways. He set his coffee down on the desk and picked up the phone. "Dr. Graves."

"Hey, Dean, it's Jason Michaels in Atlanta. How are you?"

Dr. Graves hated the use of "how are you" as a salutation. He much preferred people get to the point. But he played along with the rules of engagement. "I'm fine, Dr. Michaels. How are you?"

"Busy and discouraged, to be honest." He sighed. "More *Legionella* Tetrad cases are being reported every day. We now have reports of cases in ten counties in Georgia and at least three in neighboring states."

Dean frowned, creasing his brow. "That is not good news at all." He shook his head. "What could possibly be the source of this thing? *Legionella* outbreaks are usually—no, not usually, *always*—from a single source. But that isn't possible with the way this disease is spreading...is it? The cases are hit and miss. There's no correlation."

"My thoughts exactly," Dr. Michaels said. "We've tested the culinary water in all areas where there are cases, as well as lakes, streams, rivers, water parks, swimming pools...every possible water source we can think of. All negative."

"What can I do to help?"

"Liz said you're one of the smartest people she knows, if not *the* smartest. We need to think outside of the box here, because none of this fits into what the medical community knows about this bacteria. I need your brain power, Dean. Can you think of anything we should be looking into that we haven't already? Anything? Even if it's way out there?"

Dr. Graves rubbed his temples. His "brain power" had been running on empty as of late. Not enough sleep and the invasion of deceptive illusions into his thoughts and dreams had consumed far too much of his headspace for far too long. But no more, damnit! He would focus on this problem until he figured it out. "Let me get back to you on that. I'll be in contact if, no, *when* I have some answers or suggestions."

"Thank you, Dean. I look forward to hearing your thoughts on this." The relief in Dr. Michaels' voice made Dr. Graves worry briefly that he was putting too much faith in his defective brain, but then his confident determination from moments before returned.

"Take care, Dr. Michaels," Dean said. "And let me know if anything new comes up."

"Will do."

After hanging up, he pulled his yellow notepad over and started a list of what they knew, what water sources had been tested, and where the known cases were. He printed out a map of Georgia and each of the five states bordering it and thumbtacked it to the wall behind his desk. After a quick perusal of the daily update email sent by the CDC, he marked on the maps where the cases had appeared. Standing back against his desk, he studied them.

He didn't know Kat had come in until she said, "What are you doing?"

His heart jumped just a little, and he was proud of himself for not allowing his body to manifest the same reaction. Without turning away from the maps, he answered, "Trying to figure out this *Legionella* phenomenon. But there is no discernable pattern to this thing."

Kat came around his desk and stood beside him, staring at the maps.

"If you see anything or think of anything that might help us figure this out, speak up. And I mean *anything*, no matter how 'out there' it might seem. We're at a complete loss as to where this thing is coming from."

She nodded and leaned back against his desk. The phone rang, but neither of them moved to answer it. On the fourth ring, Kat turned and picked up the receiver. "Augusta city morgue, Kat speaking."

After listening for a moment she said, "Okay, we'll be ready." She sighed and dropped her head as she hung the phone up.

"What is it?" Dr. Graves asked.

"Another *Legionella* death." Her voice trembled just a little. "A sixteen-year-old girl. She'll be here in twenty minutes."

Dr. Graves swore under his breath and ran a hand through his hair. "We *have* to figure this out, Kat. This is unacceptable. Sixteen years old." He stared at the wall of maps for another minute then said, "Let's go get ready for her."

—⋀—

A SOMBER CORONER wheeled the body into the morgue and the three of them lifted her onto the autopsy table. He handed a packet containing the girl's medical records to Dr. Graves, nodded, and left without a word. Dr. Graves understood. What was there to say?

He and Kat worked in silence. Dr. Graves wondered briefly if Kat's mind was circling like his, trying to put the puzzle together, knowing they didn't have anywhere near enough pieces to see the whole picture.

When they finished, he took off his PPE and let the hot water run over his hands as he stood at the sink. Without looking up he said, "I don't feel like cooking tonight. And I need to get home to get Hermione from Amy's. If I order takeout would you like to come over for dinner?"

"I'd love to." Kat stepped up next to him and pumped the foaming soap into her hands.

"What do you want to eat?"

"Surprise me."

He moved out of her way, pulled two paper towels out of the dispenser, and dried his hands. He knew what to get for dinner. Back in his office he ordered takeout from Kat's favorite Chinese restaurant.

⌐∿

A LITTLE SURPRISED at his own eagerness to see the dog, *his* dog, Dean dropped the two bags of Chinese food on his kitchen island and hurried out the back door.

"I saw you pull in," Amy said as she and the two dogs climbed the few steps to his porch.

Dean couldn't hold back the grin exploding on his face as Hermione whined excitedly, wagging her tail—wagging her whole body, really—as she hurried over to him. The joy of being greeted again by a dog who had unconditional love for him seeped into his very soul. He felt like eleven-year-old Dean, being greeted by an excited Cocoa after school. Not even caring that his neighbor, whom he'd spent years trying to show only his curmudgeonly side to, stood there. "Hermione! Were you a good girl today? Did Winston play nicely with you?" He rubbed her head and scratched her back.

Winston barked once and sat at Dean's feet, looking up at him. He patted the Golden Retriever's head with his splinted hand while continuing to pet his new dog.

Amy laughed. "Well, Dr. Graves, I guess you've given in to the canine enchantment."

He tried to scowl, but his face refused. He chuckled. "I guess so. How was she today?"

"She's definitely much more well-behaved than Winston was at her age. She was no problem at all, and Winston enjoyed playing with her."

"Well, thank you so much for taking care of her for me while I'm at work. I just couldn't stand the thought of her being locked up in a crate all day."

"Me neither. And there's no need for that, I don't mind looking after her at all." She looked down at Winston. "Come on, boy. Let's go home and get dinner ready."

Hermione followed Dean into the house and went straight to her food bowl, pushing it with her nose.

"All right, girl. Hold on a minute." He scooped up a cup of dogfood and dumped it in her dish.

Watching her from behind his kitchen island, Dean got the food containers out of the two bags and set them out on the counter. As he reached in the cupboard to grab some plates, Kat let herself in the front door.

"I never got a chance to ask you today how last night went with you two." Kat nodded at the dog.

Dean laid some utensils next to the plates and stepped over to Kat. He took her by the arms and laid his forehead against hers. "I slept better than I have in...well, since I got out of the hospital after..." He changed course, not wanting bad memories to ruin what he was trying to say. "Thank you, Kat. You knew what I needed when I had no idea. And then you just acted upon it. That beautiful creature over there woke me up last night before the nightmare even had a chance to fully form. Then she laid next to me while I fell back to sleep. Falling back to sleep hasn't been a possibility for me for a while now."

"You're welcome." Kat wrapped her arms around his waist and laid her head against his chest. "I'm glad she's helping, glad you accepted my gift. I was so scared that you would be mad at me." She nearly whispered the last part.

Those words hurt Dean's heart a little. He pushed away from her so he could see her face. "Kat, look at me please."

She looked up at him, pulling at her bottom lip with her top teeth.

The vulnerability in that simple action caused tears to push against the backs of his eyes. "Kat. I'm so sorry for the way I've been behaving lately, for letting lack of sleep and...things...turn me into someone you're afraid of."

"Oh, Dean," she interrupted. "I'm not afraid of *you*. I know you would—"

He placed a finger on her lips, his turn to interrupt. "I'm sorry my mood swings have been making you feel like you have to walk on eggshells around me. So very sorry, Kat. Please forgive me."

He stopped the abuse her nervous teeth were perpetrating on her lip the only he knew how. He pulled her close and kissed her.

ELEVEN

By Friday morning, Dean and Hermione had developed a routine. Each morning Dean felt a little jolt of jealousy at the excitement the dog displayed when time came to take her next door. But each evening when he picked her up after work, she rewarded him with at least double the tail-wags and exultant whines than she'd shown for her dog-friend, Winston.

Dean smiled and waved at Amy before heading down her porch steps and to his car next door. Last night had been the first night since getting her that Hermione hadn't needed to wake him up. He'd dreamed, but it was a normal, far from nightmarish, dream. He drew in a deep breath of the fresh morning air before getting in his car, relishing the lingering scent of rain from a cloudburst during the night.

A full night's rest was a heavenly thing—and one Dean would never take for granted again. Not wanting to spoil his good mood, he switched his radio from the usual news station to an oldies station, humming along to the James Taylor song playing there. After picking up two coffees at the drive-thru, he pulled into the parking lot at the morgue, smiling again as he parked next to Kat's car.

Kat stood just inside the employee entrance, waiting for the elevator. She turned to him, her smile widening as her gaze dropped to the aromatic cups in his hands. She took one from him and sniffed at the steam before leaning in, rising to her tip-toes, and kissing him on the cheek. "Thank you."

He looked from side to side, habitually checking to make sure no one had observed him in a less than professional moment. "You're—"

Face flushing, Kat interrupted, "I'm sorry, Dr. Graves. I forgot myself for a minute when I smelled this much-needed beverage."

His shoulders slumped a little and a mild feeling of nausea rippled through his stomach. Refusing his body's inclination to search his surroundings again, Dean lifted Kat's chin and waited for her gaze to meet his. He spoke softly, tamping down the emotions threatening to flood his mind. "Kat, I'm the one who's sorry."

"But I—"

He shook his head. "You did nothing wrong. I'm sorry my rigid rules about professionalism, my rigidness in general, have made you second-guess your natural, beautiful responses. I will work on being more flexible." The elevator door opened, and they stepped inside. "And," he continued, "I've decided I don't care who knows about us, about the way I feel about you." He cleared his throat and looked down. "Just, maybe, not the detectives."

Kat's musical laughter tickled his ears in just the right way. She scooted closer to him and leaned her head against his shoulder. "I will keep it professional at work, especially in front of Davis and Fitzpatrick. I don't want to break you."

The door slid open. Dean reached for Kat's arm to stop her from exiting. She looked up at him with a cocked eyebrow and, throwing all caution to the wind, he bent down and kissed her right on the lips, lingering a few seconds longer than he meant to, the hint of her French vanilla coffee converging between them. When the elevator started to close, he pulled away and inserted his splinted hand between the doors so they opened again, then gestured for a smiling Kat to exit first.

"Well, Dr. Graves," she said as she scanned her ID badge to open the door to the morgue, "you've surprised me this morning."

His pulse quickened, whether because of the kiss itself or because he'd dared kiss her in a semi-public space, he wasn't sure. Either way, it was shaping up to be a good day.

His cell phone buzzed in his pocket. He switched hands with his coffee, holding it between his thumb and first two fingers that weren't wrapped up in the splint, then dug in his pocket for the vibrating phone. "Dr. Graves," he answered.

"Graves, Fitzpatrick here."

Clenching his jaw, he corrected the detective for the millionth time. "It's *Doctor* Graves, detective. What do you need?" He would try to relax with Kat around the office, but there were just some things he wouldn't budge on.

"Yeah, uhh, sorry"—he didn't sound at all sorry—"I just wanted to give you a heads-up that we're sending you a stiff."

"Detective Fitzpatrick, that is disrespectful and I won't tolerate it. Start over." Where was Detective Rodriguez? She wouldn't disrespect the dead like that. He hoped she hadn't gone back to her own precinct already.

After an exaggerated sigh, Fitzpatrick said, "*Dr.* Graves, we have a case for you, as per the coroner from the Sheriff's department. The *deceased* is a fifty-three-year-old female, witnessed arrest at a restaurant. She and two friends had just been seated. The waiter brought water to the table, the deceased took a small drink of it then set it back on the table. The waiter cracked a joke and the three ladies laughed. The deceased started coughing, holding a fist up to her mouth. Between bouts of coughing she choked out 'breathed in' and then 'own spit'. She continued to cough, eyes were watering. According to witnesses, she seemed fine, shaking her head and laughing a little. Then she started to look worried, turned pale, seemed to be unable to breathe at all, lips turned blue. It was at this point that one of her friends called 9-1-1. The deceased lost consciousness and when EMS arrived had no respiratory effort or pulse. Attempts to resuscitate failed."

"What are the coroner's thoughts?" Dr. Graves asked.

"He has no idea. She was fine, healthy previous to this episode. He knows it's unlikely, but wants to make sure there was nothing in the water that may have caused this, or nothing that she may have ingested earlier that caused it."

"Okay. Thank you, Detective Fitzpatrick. What is the ETA?"

A muffled voice came across the phone, like the detective had covered the mouthpiece and was talking to someone at the scene. "Sorry, Dr. Graves," Fitzpatrick said after several seconds. "The ambulance is bringing the body now. Should be there in less than five minutes."

"Thanks for the heads-up," Dr. Graves quipped.

"Sorry, busy morning. I'll bring in my report after I finish gathering the witness statements."

"See you then." Dr. Graves ended the call and shoved the phone back in his pocket before switching his coffee back to that hand.

Kat had listened in on his side of the conversation. "I'll go set my stuff in my office then get things ready." She started down the hallway then stopped and looked back. "This isn't another *Legionella* case, is it?"

"No. I'm not really sure what it is, but I'm relatively certain it isn't *Legionella* that caused this woman's death."

Nodding, Kat continued to her office.

—∿—

DR. GRAVES LEFT his hand splint on his desk. It no longer hurt as bad to pull on tight surgical gloves. The medics had removed the deceased from the body bag for him and handed their chart to Kat. Then they lingered. Which was unlike most medics. Especially at this time of day, the beginning of a twenty-four-hour shift when most of them just wanted to go grab a bite to eat while they had a chance.

"Is there anything else?" Dr. Graves asked.

The dark-haired medic whose nametag said E. Geary, shrugged and looked from the doctor to Kat. "We're just kind of wondering if there have been any leads on what's causing this deadly pneumonia. Like, if you know or suspect anything the media isn't reporting."

Dr. Graves didn't blame them for asking. They were on the front lines of this and had a right to know if they were at risk. "I'm afraid not. There seems to be little correlation between victims. We can't even determine a source at this point. I'm sorry. I wish I knew more."

The medics nodded and E. Geary said, "Thanks, doc. I just thought I'd ask."

"No harm in asking." Dr. Graves ignored the "doc," he knew the medic hadn't said it to get on his nerves like Pup and Davis. "One good thing is that it doesn't seem to spread through respirations, so you all should be pretty safe on that front."

The medics both released a relieved breath. E. Geary said, "Thanks. That helps." He waved and smiled at Kat, saying, "Catch you later."

"Bye Emmitt," Kat responded absently as she concentrated on entering the deceased's information into the computer.

Dean watched the medics wheel their stretcher into the elevator. "How do you know him?"

"I was engaged to him."

Whipping his head around to look at her, Dean smacked it against the exam light hanging above the autopsy table. He bit down on the curse he almost uttered and what came out instead was a combination "*oomph-ouch-shi...*"

Kat snorted as she attempted to hold in a laugh. "Are you okay?"

"I'm fine." He glared at the exam light like it was a sentient being that had purposefully rapped him upside the head. He turned to look at Kat. "So...you, uhh..."

With a roll of her eyes and a shake of her head, Kat said, "I was just joking, Dr. Graves. I've never been engaged. Emmitt and I suffered through the city's week-long new employee orientation together when I first started here. I've only run into him two or three times in the last few years since then."

The muscles of his shoulders and upper back released the tension he hadn't known he held there. "Well"—he cleared his throat—"I wouldn't have been upset or anything if it were true. Just a little surprised that I didn't know."

Kat's mouth turned up into that charming little smirk she always got when teasing him—the one that made her eyes light up in a way he adored even though it was almost always as his expense. "There are many things you don't yet know about me, Dr. Graves. But being previously engaged isn't one of them."

He smiled as he turned back to the body lying on the table. He looked forward to finding out those "many things" in the days to come. Kat's fingers clicked on the keyboard of the bedside computer as she returned to the job at hand. Dr. Graves drew in a deep breath and held it for a few seconds while he shifted his mindset to autopsy-mode. He donned gloves and worked in silence as he cut off the deceased's clothing, depositing each item in a separate paper bag laid out previously by Kat.

After switching on the head-smacking exam light, he adjusted it to shine on the woman's face. He tapped on the foot control to start the audio recording and began to dictate the findings of his cursory exam. "Upon initial exam of this fifty-three-year-old female, cyanosis is noted over the face, lips, and fingertips. Petechial hemorrhages on eyelids and face."

Dr. Graves gently pried open the woman's mouth and after inspecting it, moved to her eyes, pulling down the lower lids to inspect the conjunctiva. He continued his dictation. "Petechial hemorrhages seen in bilateral conjunctiva and oral mucosa. Facial and conjunctival congestion present."

He turned the microphone off and proceeded to draw blood samples from the femoral vein. After handing the samples to Kat to label and process, he said, "Are you ready to assist with the autopsy? I'll decide which lab and toxicology tests to order after we're done."

She nodded. "Give me a minute to get my PPE on."

—⋀—

"WHAT DO YOU SEE HERE?" Dr. Graves pointed to the pleura lining the outside of the woman's lungs.

"It looks like petechiae," she looked up at him, "right?"

"Exactly." He made the appropriate cuts to remove the heart and handed it to Kat to weigh while he worked on removing the lungs.

After weighing the heart and then each lung, Kat recorded the numbers then stood next to Dr. Graves as he dissected the lungs, watching intently.

He clicked on the dictation microphone. "Lungs have a spongy consistency. Blood-stained fluid was expressed from the parenchyma upon compression, indicating acute congestion. Small tissue samples taken from both lungs for microscopic evaluation."

When the microphone was once again turned off, Kat asked, "What could that mean? The congestion?"

"There are many causes of pulmonary congestion, but in this case, I suspect negative thoracic pressure caused when the victim was trying to inhale against some sort of blockage."

"What could have been blocking her airway? We didn't find any foreign bodies, her epiglottis wasn't swollen. You said everything looked normal during the neck dissection."

"The only thing I can think of is that she aspirated—likely on her own saliva, since that's what she said before her airway closed off— and the coughing and aspiration triggered a sustained laryngospasm that prevented her from inhaling or exhaling."

Kat's eyes widened, and she swallowed. "Is that common? Dying from inhaling your own spit?"

"No. Not at all. I've never even heard of a case where that was the determined cause. Most laryngospasms, though frightening, resolve on their own within minutes and don't cause complete blockage. She may have had an underlying issue, but not something I could see upon inspection of her vocal cords or other throat anatomy."

"How are you going to prove or rule it out?"

"I may not be able to definitively. It will likely boil down to the eyewitness accounts, negative toxicology report, and correlating tissue pathology. But I'm fairly certain I'll be listing the cause of death as 'findings consistent with asphyxiation secondary to laryngospasm'."

"So," Kat raised her eyebrows, "really, death by inhaling her own spit."

Dr. Graves nodded. "That appears to be the case."

"So random," Kat said.

TWELVE

For the first time in months, Dr. Graves got his easel and paints out. He'd forgotten how much joy it brought him to position a fresh canvas on the easel. He'd ditched the hand splint—hopefully for good—after brushing his immobilized fingers across a freshly painted flower petal.

Kat and Hermione had joined him to spend Saturday hiking trails in north Augusta, with the dog playing in water any chance she got. It had been a full day that ended with takeout on the patio as they watched the sunset.

Today, however, Kat stayed home to get caught up on housework and laundry, and Dean had decided to spend the afternoon enjoying his favorite hobby he'd neglected for too long. He breathed in the mild aroma of the paint and hummed as he watched Hermione and Winston wrestle on the lawn. A few colors mixed on his pallet created the perfect shade for the seed area of the sunflower he was working on. He couldn't help but smile as he recalled Kat's squeal of delight when they'd come upon a field of the flowers in full bloom. Apparently, they were her favorite flower.

His phone buzzed behind him where it sat on the small table between the two Adirondack chairs. Dean finished a few more strokes with his paintbrush before turning to grab it.

"Dr. Graves," he said as he pressed the phone to his ear.

"Dean, do you have a minute to talk?" As usual, the infectious disease doctor did not identify himself.

"Hi, Dr. Shah. I have as much time as you need. What's going on?"

"I'm really sorry to call you on a Sunday, but I want to get your take on this." He paused, shuffling papers in the background. "Between us here at Augusta U, and Doctors Hospital, we've had five men admitted in the last forty-eight hours with probable *Legionella* Tetrad."

"Five?" Dr. Graves ran a hand through his hair as he paced. "Any connections to each other?"

"Yes, as a matter of fact, there is a connection this time."

Dr. Graves stopped pacing and stiffened. "What is it?"

"They all attended the same gym within two days of becoming ill. I don't have all the details because I haven't had time to track anything down—and won't have time in the foreseeable future—but I thought you might. The thing I find most odd is that there were actually more women than men attending the gym in that time period, and none of them are showing any symptoms."

Mind now racing like a super-genius on the verge of a great discovery, Dr. Graves asked, "Which gym?"

"It's called Energy Zone. I'm not sure of the address—"

"I can look it up. Thanks, Romit." He ended the call without asking if Dr. Shah had anything else to tell him.

Dr. Graves called the gym and asked to speak to the owner—who happened to be the only one there since the health department had shut the gym down until they figured things out. The owner was more than happy to meet with him, he'd do whatever was needed to safely reopen. Pacing again, Dr. Graves asked Siri for the address of Energy Zone then sent it to his phone's map.

As he headed toward the door into his house, he looked up and bit back a curse. He'd forgotten about his paints and his dog.

He dialed Kat and held the phone to his ear with his shoulder as he cleaned up his paints.

"Hello?" Kat answered.

"Hello, Kat. Can I bring Hermione over for a bit? I have a lead on the *Legionella* outbreak and I need to go investigate." The words spilled from his mouth rapid-fire as he tucked his satchel of paints under his arm and lifted the partially finished painting from the easel, carrying it with one hand while he held the brushes in the other. "Come on, Hermione. Inside." He held the storm door open with his foot as the dog slid past him into the house.

"Dean." Kat's voice came out an octave higher than usual. "What, exactly, are you investigating?"

He dropped the satchel on the kitchen counter and laid the canvas on the island. "I'll explain when I get to your house to drop off Hermione...that is, if you're okay to watch her." He scowled at the paintbrushes in his hand. He didn't have time to properly clean them.

Kat breathed in and out a couple of times before answering. "I don't mind watching her. I just...I don't want..." Another deep breath and her voice came back a little wobbly, like she was upset—or trying not to cry. "Dean. Do I need to be worried about you?"

That stopped him in his somewhat manic tracks. Ooh. That was why the wobbly voice. The last time he'd taken on an investigative role in a case hadn't turned out so well. He closed his eyes and pinched the bridge of his nose. How unthoughtful of him to spring this on her like that. "Kat, I'm sorry. I didn't mean to make you worry. It's nothing even remotely dangerous. Can I explain when I get there?"

Her voice only slightly less tinged with concern, she replied, "Yes. See you in a few minutes."

Grabbing a handful of zip-lock bags from his cupboard, Dean placed each brush in its own bag, pressed as much air out as he could, and zipped it shut. He pressed his lips together. It probably wouldn't save the brushes, but it was worth a try. He'd clean them as soon as he got home. He pulled his painter's smock off and hung it over a chair.

Hermione danced in front of him at the sight of her leash being taken off the peg where it hung, her claws clicking against the hardwood in his kitchen.

Dean gave the command for her to sit before clipping the leash to her collar. "Let's go see Kat, shall we?"

The wiggle dance started again. The excitement just too much for the young dog to control. Dean laughed. "I feel that way about seeing her too."

—⋏—

KAT MET Dean and the dog on the porch with a weak smile. The scent of fresh laundry wafted out from the open door as Kat reached down to greet Hermione with a rub to her furry neck.

"I guess it was to be expected," Dean said with a shake of his head.

"What?" Kat asked as she straightened up and looked him in the eye.

Dean shrugged. "That I'd end up coming in second to Hermione."

Kat rolled her eyes then threw her arms around his neck in a tight embrace. "She is less of a troublemaker than you."

He really couldn't argue that.

"Come in." Kat released her iron grip and held the door open. "Ignore the laundry lying all over the couch, I wanted to watch Avengers as I folded."

"Good choice." He knelt to unhook the leash from Hermione's collar once inside.

"So," Kat said, hands on hips. "Where are you going and what are you investigating?"

Dean explained about the new cases and that they all came from the same gym. "I'm just going to the gym to see what I can find out from the owner, he's meeting me there. I have the beginnings of a hypothesis forming, and I want to check a couple of things out."

"Isn't that dangerous? What if you get the disease?"

"I won't. The gym is closed down for now and we're just going to be meeting in the owner's office."

Kat folded her arms and raised an eyebrow at him.

He sighed. "I'll take an N-95 mask with me, in case I have an uncontrollable urge to explore."

—∿—

TRUE TO HIS WORD, Dr. Graves stopped at the morgue to grab an N-95 mask before driving to the gym on the other end of town. During the fifteen-minute drive, he catalogued the theories that had been running loose in his head since the call from Dr. Shah, weighing them against each other and what he knew.

The privately owned gym was bigger than he'd expected. Almost as big as the nationwide chain over by the Target. The owner met him at the door, partially blocking the sign taped to it that read "CLOSED by order of the Georgia Department of Health." His shaved white scalp glistened with tiny beads of sweat as he thrust his hand out toward Dr. Graves for a handshake. "Dr. Graves, it's good to meet you. I'm Dave Hawkes, owner of Energy Zone."

"Mind if we just fist-bump?" Dr. Graves asked. "I'm a bit of a germaphobe."

Dave curled his outstretched hand into a fist and bumped it against Dr. Graves' with a nod. "I bet you are. Probably comes with the territory of your profession."

Dr. Graves wasn't so sure about that, he'd hated touching other people since long before becoming a medical examiner. "Mind if we go inside? I have some questions I'd like to ask you."

"Sure, sure. Of course." He gestured for the doctor to go through the door ahead of him while he held it open. "My office is just over there, to the right, behind the front desk."

The office was messy but somewhat organized, pictures of a younger Dave holding various trophies plastered the walls. Weight training or fitness competitions, Dr. Graves assumed.

"Have a seat." The owner gestured to a chair in front of his desk.

Dean sat on the edge of the chair, too anxious to relax back into it. "Mr. Hawkes," he started right in. "As I told you on the phone, I, along with several government agencies, have been trying to figure out what is causing this *Legionella* Tetrad outbreak—and I think we might finally find some answers here, in your gym."

"Welp, I sure hope y'all do. But why do you think you'll find answers here?"

"This is the first instance where there is a close correlation of the disease infecting multiple patients that have a common, *possible* common, origin of the disease."

"But wait, wasn't there an outbreak in Atlanta at an apartment building?" His high forehead wrinkled with a frown.

"Correct," Dr. Graves nodded. "However, the patients had no contact with each other or access to apartments other than their own. Here," he gestured toward the rows of gym equipment visible through the office's open door, "we may be able to figure out a common source."

"How? The health department already took water samples and swabbed all the equipment the clients remembered using. What else are you suggesting?"

Dean leaned forward. "I'm just going to ask you some questions. I have a couple of theories that can either be disproven or merit further investigation depending on the answers."

"Okay. Shoot."

"My first question is in response to the fact that all the infected from this site are male, even though an equal number, or more, of your patrons are female. This should help us narrow it down. Where would men congregate, but not women?"

Dave wiped his bald head with a tissue. "They use all the same equipment, classrooms, pool. The only areas that aren't co-ed are the dressing rooms and showers, and the saunas."

Dr. Graves nodded, smiling. "Exactly what I was thinking. See? We've already narrowed it down to three areas."

"Well, really two areas." Dave grinned. "The dressing rooms and showers are connected."

"Good, good." The doctor took a moment to arrange his thoughts. "Is there anything you can think of in those places that is or would have been different between the men's and the women's areas?"

"Different how?" He picked up a pen and began tapping it on his desk.

"Like, different water sources, cleaners, or filters in the drinking fountains or something. Anything you can think of."

Dave shook his head, a deep crease forming between his eyebrows as he stared straight ahead at nothing. He tapped the pen on the desk faster, then stopped and stood, dropping the pen. "The showerheads." He turned his head toward Dr. Graves and met his gaze. "We just installed new showerheads in the men's showers Wednesday night."

"Not in the women's?"

"No, sir. We have the new ones back in the storage room, but my maintenance guy hasn't gotten around to installing them yet."

"Mr. Hawkes, do you happen to know if any or all of the affected men took showers after the installation?"

"Yeah." He nodded. "I don't really know one of the guys, but the other four are regulars and always shower after they work out."

THIRTEEN

D r. Graves paced in front of the gym, phone held to his ear. First, he'd called Kat to tell her he'd be a little longer and there was nothing to worry about, he'd fill her in later. Now he waited, counting the number of times the phone rang before Tracey answered.

"Four, five—"

"Dean, why are you calling me on a Sunday?" Tracey's irritated voice blared in his ear over what sounded like a raucous party in the background.

"Tracey. I think I have a lead on the *Legionella* Tetrad epidemic."

"And again, why are you calling me? This is a health department issue, not a police issue."

Ignoring her annoyance, he explained, "It's possible that it's both. I'll call them too, but right now, I need you to send your CSI people to Energy Zone. I'll send you the address. Or do you want the health department to mess up any evidence that might be here? Chain of custody? Do you want a possible bioterrorist to continue to roam free in Georgia?"

Tracey sighed. "Okay. I'm sorry for being short with y'all instead of thankful. This gives me a good excuse to leave my husband's family reunion. I'll get CSI on their way, and I'll be right behind them. Send me the coordinates." She ended the call.

Dr. Graves looked at his phone and mumbled, "By 'coordinates' I hope you just mean the address, chief." He texted her the address.

—⋀—

After explaining things to Megan, the crime scene investigator, and Chief Billings, Dr. Graves spelled out what he was thinking. "Evidence suggests the five cases that possibly—probably—originated from here, are somehow related to the installation of five new showerheads in the men's dressing room."

"But surely more than just five men have showered between Thursday morning and when the health department shut the gym down this morning," Chief Billings said.

"I know." Dr. Graves ran a hand through his hair. "I've thought about that, and I don't have an answer for it yet. But the correlation is still there and we need to act on that."

Megan nodded. "Right. I'll start by getting water samples directly from those five showerheads and then from the older showerheads in the women's dressing room as the control. I also think we should take the showerheads themselves—the new ones—for testing."

"Yes," Dr. Graves agreed. "Both the five already installed and the unused ones in the storage room that were bought at the same time. Oh, and, please collect two of each sample so we can send one by courier to Atlanta."

"Definitely." Megan looked from him to the chief of police.

Tracey gave the young investigator a curt nod. "Go get started then. I'll need to talk to Mr. Hawkes when he's done showing you the facilities."

"What are you going to talk to him about?" Dr. Graves asked Tracey as Megan and the gym owner walked away.

"Well, if the focus at this point is those showerheads, I'm going to find out where he got them." She popped a mint into her mouth and moved it to the side with her tongue. "Why don't you go on home, Dean? I got this now."

"Thanks, Tracey." He nodded. "I need to go call the folks in Atlanta. See you soon."

"Yep."

—∿—

Dr. Graves waited until he was back at Kat's to make the call to Drs. Allen and Michaels—mostly because he wanted Kat to hear what he'd found out, but also because he needed her help to set up a three-way call on his phone. He hated to bother them on the weekend, but chances were that at least Dr. Michaels was already working if not Liz also.

He put his phone on speaker and set it on Kat's counter. He rubbed Hermione's fur as he told them about the gym and his theory about the bacteria and the showers.

"So, what exactly are you thinking, Dean?" Liz asked.

"I'm not sure how yet, but I think the bacteria is coming from the showerheads. We'll know more after CSI gets some results back."

Dr. Michaels asked, "And you did say that you told the crime scene investigator to collect samples for the health department, too?"

"Yes."

"Do you happen to know where they plan to send those samples? To your local health department or to us here in Atlanta?"

Dr. Graves answered, "For you. The health department here already obtained their own samples."

"Perfect. Do you think we could get one each of the used and unused new showerheads too?"

"Yes. I'll give Chief Billings a call when we're done here."

"What else would you suggest we do on our end?" Liz asked.

"If you can, I suggest you test the water coming directly from the showerheads of the victims from the new apartment building. And, maybe have the contact tracers call the other victims' families and ask about any new bathroom fixtures. I wouldn't specify showerheads at this point, as it may end up being more or other fixtures than just those."

"And if they did have new fixtures?" Jason asked.

"Then we get the detectives involved to ask more questions, like, who installed them? Where did they buy them from? What brand are they?"

"That makes sense."

"Anything else?" Liz asked.

"No, but if I think of anything, I'll let you know. You two do likewise," Dr. Graves said. "And I'll share the test results with you as soon as I get them."

"Same here," Jason said, adding, "Thank you, Dr. Graves. This is the first real break we've had as to where this thing might be coming from."

"No need to thank me, this is a team effort. Talk to you soon." Dr. Graves ended the call and looked at the time display on his phone then up at Kat. "I'm starving. Do you want to go get a bite to eat?"

"How about we just make some sandwiches and hang out here? I went shopping this morning." She grinned. He'd made fun of her in the past about never having any good food in her house. "I even bought your favorite chips."

"That sounds perfect." He gave in to the overwhelming urge to kiss her. They pulled apart, both laughing when Dean's stomach growled.

⌁

AFTER CHECKING the daily update email sent to the group by the CDC, Dr. Graves added the new *Legionella* cases to the maps on his office wall first thing Monday morning. Other than the gym and the apartment building, the infections were occurring in a chaotic, scattered pattern. He leaned against the back of his chair, studying the maps. If his theory proved correct, that would explain some of the randomness, but it would elicit new questions—as scientific theory often did.

His desk phone rang, startling him out of his deep thoughts. He reached behind him to answer it, still facing the maps on the wall. "Dr. Graves."

"Hi, Dr. Graves. This is Jason Michaels. I thought you'd want to know that we got the results back from the gym water."

"Already?" Dr. Graves was more accustomed to the snail's pace of the crime lab than the rapidity with which the medical community received results.

"Yes. Well, at least the PCR tests they ran, there are other tests pending."

"What did they find?"

"You were right! The water from the in-use showerhead had a low positive for *Legionella,* but the crazy results were from the still-packaged, unused showerhead they were planning on putting in the women's showers."

People who paused for dramatic effect exasperated Dr. Graves. "And that was…?"

"The 'alert' level for *Legionella* in water systems is one-thousand genomic units, or GUs, per liter, and the 'action' level is ten-thousand GUs per liter. The water obtained by running sterile water through the unused showerhead came back at greater than two-hundred-thousand GUs."

"Wow." Dr. Graves stood straighter, no longer leaning against his chair. "What was the number for the 'low positive' on the men's showerheads?"

"Less than a thousand."

"And water samples from other areas of the gym?"

"All negative."

"So it *is* the showerheads." Dr. Graves finally turned from the maps, pulled his chair out, and sat at his desk, pulling a yellow legal pad to him. He wrote, *bacteria dissipates to low levels after one use of showerhead. What does this mean about intentions?*

"Dr. Graves?" Dr. Michaels' voice through the phone pressed to Dr. Graves' ear by his shoulder reminded him he hadn't finished the conversation with the Georgia Department of Health doctor.

"Oh, uhh, sorry. Just trying to organize my thoughts."

"Perfect segue for my next question—what *are* your thoughts?"

"At the forefront is the probability, from what we know, that only one person gets sick per showerhead—or, to better state it, one infective dose per showerhead. After that, the bacteria seems to be washed out to non-infective levels."

"I thought the same thing. What else?"

Dr. Graves shook his head, dislodging the phone from its perch on his shoulder. It clunked to his desk. He winced and picked it up. "Sorry, I dropped the phone. I hope I didn't blow out your eardrum."

Jason laughed. "Nope. Tympanic membrane is still intact."

"Good. My other thoughts are centered around why. Why would someone purposefully do this? Did they mean to make it so it diminished after one use? Is it just a big accident? I can't see it being an accident, what with the four different types of *Legionella* involved. And then—how? How is this person getting it into the showerheads? What about other bathroom or kitchen fixtures?" Dr. Graves stopped and took a breath. "As you can see, I have many thoughts and questions."

"As do I. I'm hoping we have at least a little more clarification this afternoon. The contact tracers are going to start calling the families and friends of previous patients at nine to ask about their showerhead situations. I'll let you know what they find out."

"And I'll let you know if the investigation turns anything up here." Dr. Graves said an absent goodbye and hung up, back to writing on his note pad before the phone even settled in the cradle.

FOURTEEN

"So, Dean, what does this mean?" Chief Billings sat across his desk from him, CSI report in her hand.

"Right now it means we should collect the showerheads from all the victims' homes and find out when they were installed and where they were purchased, manufactured, who installed them—any information we can get."

"And by 'we' you mean the police, right?" She narrowed her gaze at him.

"Yes, of course." He looked away from her. She still hadn't completely forgiven him for taking the huge risks he'd taken with the Ridge case. "But...will you please keep me in the loop? We need to figure this out before more victims succumb."

"That I will," she said. "Without your brain we wouldn't even be this far."

"I just thought of something I forgot to ask Dr. Michaels, maybe you know the answer. Was there any fluid found in the new, unused showerheads when they removed them from the packaging?"

"Megan thought about that too. She said there was not even a trace of moisture anywhere she could see or swab."

"Dr. Graves, Chief Billings," Kat said as she stuck her head through the doorway. "You might want to turn on the News at Noon."

Nausea shot through Dr. Graves' insides. "Come in and have a seat, Kat." He found the website, clicked on the top story, and turned his monitor at an angle they could all see.

"The mysterious illness and deaths of young and old from what the health department is calling *Legionella* Tetrad, has hit Augusta with a punch." The camera panned to a wide shot, showing the cute young reporter standing in front of Energy Zone, balancing on impossibly high-heeled shoes. "News at Noon has discovered that the five most recent cases of the deadly pneumonia may have originated here, at this gym behind me."

The camera shifted to show the owner of the gym standing a few feet to the reporter's left. "I have here the owner of Energy Zone, Dave Hawkes, and he's agreed to talk to us about what he knows." She turned to him. "Mr. Hawkes, thank you for speaking with us."

"It's my pleasure."

"I understand the health department and the police were here this weekend. What did they find?" She tilted her head and adopted that concerned look all reporters must learn in school.

"I don't know for sure, but they sure were interested in some new showerheads we installed in the men's showers—the medical examiner, Dr. Graves, was the one to first ask about those. The cops took them and some others, took water samples, asked a million questions." He folded his arms, accentuating his biceps.

The reporter's eyes bulged when he mentioned Dean. "Dr. Graves? Of the Bar Killer infamy?"

Dr. Graves groaned at hearing his name.

"Yeah!" Dave wagged a finger in front of him. "That's where I recognized him from!"

She nodded, appearing to make a mental note, and continued with her line of questioning. "Tell me about these showerheads. Do they think they've found a source for this disease?"

Dave shrugged. "Maybe. Like I said, they sure were interested in those showers."

"Thank you, Mr. Hawkes, for speaking with us." She turned to face the camera, and the view shifted to a closeup of her face and shoulders. "There you have it. It seems that there may soon be a break in this case of what some are referring to as an act of bioterrorism. We'll be sure to keep you updated on the latest developments here on News at Noon."

Dr. Graves exited the site, turned his monitor back to face him, and dropped his head. "I really wish that guy wouldn't have brought up my name." He sighed and looked up. "Well, is this going to help us or hurt us with this investigation, Tracey?"

She shrugged. "You never know. It could bring out the crazies and conspiracy theorists, or people that really know something. Likely all of the above."

The three of them sat in contemplative silence for a moment before Chief Billings stood with a grunt. "I'd better get back to the precinct. I can't leave those guys alone for very long, they're like a bunch of toddlers."

—⋏—

THE NEXT MORNING Dr. Graves sipped coffee at his desk and opened his email. The daily message from the CDC showed no new cases. Thankfully. He set the coffee down and tilted his head as he noticed the subject line of the next email. *Legionella Expert*. He didn't recognize the AOL address it had come from: AMscienceislife. Dean figured it wouldn't hurt to open it as long as he didn't click on any links.

Dr. Graves,

My name is Andrew Matheson, PhD. I am a microbiologist with an extensive curriculum vitae. I graduated from Harvard, Summa Cum Laude, at the top of my class. I do not tell you this to be self-aggrandizing, only to convey to you my qualifications.

I find myself currently on a sabbatical from the daily rigors of research and the like. And I am bored and in need of distraction, thus this email. I saw on the news that the origin of this plague that has befallen many in our great state of Georgia may have been narrowed down to, of all things, certain bathroom fixtures. I would like to volunteer my time and expertise to assist in uncovering the mysteries of this Legionella outbreak, if you will have me.

If teaming up is something you are interested in, I propose that we meet at the Starbucks on Washington Road this Friday at noon.

Please RSVP by 5:00 tonight. If I do not hear from you by then, I will assume that you are not interested.

Sincerely,

Dr. Andrew Matheson, PhD

Dr. Graves opened a search engine and typed in "Andrew Matheson, microbiology." If this man truly was who he said, his credentials passed the internet stalking challenge. There was a Harvard graduate microbiologist with that name. He scrolled down and clicked on a CDC newsletter from several years ago announcing the hiring of Dr. Andrew Matheson as the assistant lead microbiologist.

"Hmm," Dr. Graves said.

"Hmm what?" Kat stopped in his doorway.

He explained the email and showed her what his search had turned up. "What do you think? Should I meet with him?"

She stiffened a little then rolled her shoulders before answering. "I think *we* should meet with him. Both of us. It should be pretty safe in a public place like Starbucks."

Dean reached across his desk and touched her arm. "Okay. We'll meet with him together."

Kat nodded and squeezed his hand. "Do you think it's legit?"

He shrugged. "It could just be someone posing as this scientist, but the wording of the email makes me think he's the real deal. I hope he is, maybe he'll be able to shed some light on this seemingly impossible bacteria."

FIFTEEN

Dean was up early Thursday morning. Having his name broadcast on a news program must have triggered...something. Even though he'd had to admit to himself that he—probably—had PTSD, he still had a hard time using the term, even in his own mind. Thank heavens for Hermione. She'd awakened him at least three times throughout the night just as nightmares began to invade. The last time, he looked at his alarm clock and 4:32 glared back at him, so he just got up.

Not wanting to go into work that early, he showered and got dressed in jeans and a t-shirt, then took Hermione for a walk around the neighborhood in the pre-dawn light of the moon. He led the dog onto a dirt path that meandered through a large copse of trees. About twenty yards in, something rustled in the underbrush just off the trail. Dean stopped, a chill running the length of his body as Hermione stiffened and growled beside him.

"Probably just a rodent of some sort," he whispered. He remained frozen in place, unable to decide if he should turn around and head out of the trees—thus turning his back on whatever lay hidden nearby —or forge ahead and get past it. Or...what? Stand here like a woolly mammoth frozen in ice for millions of years?

Hermione made the decision for them when she barked and bounded toward the sound, pulling the leash out of Dean's hand. "Hermione! No!"

The dog stuck her nose into a bush, and an orange cat vaulted out the other side and scrambled up the nearest tree. With one more short bark at the base of the tree, Hermione turned and loped back to him with a proud gleam in her doggy eyes.

Dean looked from her up to the cat hanging onto a thin branch, its hair standing on end, hissing down at them. It definitely did not seem like a tame, household pet. Probably feral. Did cats really get stuck in trees? Dean shook his head and got his feet moving again, walking back to civilization and streetlamps. Maybe he'd come back and check on the cat after work when the sun was out.

―⋁―

THE SUN ROSE as he drove to the morgue. His phone buzzed while he was still two blocks away and he let it go to voicemail instead of trying to dig it out of his pocket while driving. As soon as he parked, he checked the message.

"Hello, Dr. Graves. This is Isabella Rodriguez. I wanted to give you a heads-up before I go off shift about the body that should be waiting for you when you get in this morning. Nineteen-year-old male found dead in his dorm room when his roommate returned from a date at around one A.M. The roommate was using the screen of his cellphone as a light so he didn't wake the victim up, so the lighting was sparse. He kicked his flip-flops off and proceeded down the middle of the small room toward his desk positioned near the head of the bed. A few steps in, he felt something wet and sticky on the carpet." She paused and what sounded like a yawn came over the recording. "Sorry, long night. So the roommate stepped in something wet and sticky, the next step was also wet, when he reached the desk, he turned his lamp on. And...blood everywhere. Roommate took one look at the deceased and knew he was dead, called 9-1-1, and, well, here we are. I'll email the CSI photos and my full report to you and Ms. Flanagan before I head home. Not sure if this was something accidental or a crime scene. There didn't appear to be a struggle. Call if you need more info."

Young guy, a lot of blood, no apparent struggle—accident or

crime? Or, he frowned, suicide? Intriguing. This young man's family deserved an answer. Dr. Graves went over how he would proceed with this autopsy as he walked to the building and rode the elevator down to the morgue. The coroner's report sat on the autopsy table. Dr. Graves picked it up and switched the computer on so it would be booted up by the time Kat got there—he looked up at the clock—which should be any minute. He walked to the wall of refrigerated drawers and looked at the sign-in sheet. The deceased had arrived at 0315 and was in drawer six.

Dr. Graves pulled the drawer open and wheeled the transport gurney over to it. As he was setting the brakes, Kat stepped through the doors.

"Let me go set my stuff down in my office and I'll come help you," she said.

"Thank you." He watched her disappear down the hallway, emotions warring inside him—sadness at the death of this young person before him and a grateful serenity that Kat was in his life.

"What do we have?" Kat asked as they lifted the body bag onto the transport gurney.

He explained what he knew as they set up for the autopsy.

After removing the body from the bag, Dr. Graves stood back and examined the whole picture. He looked up at Kat and asked, "Will you please check your email to see if Detective Rodriguez sent her report?"

She clicked some keys then said, "Yes, it's here."

"Look and see if there was any drug paraphernalia found at the scene. I'm not sure we'll be able to pull much blood for toxicology so I'll have to send other tissue samples for that."

Kat scrolled through the report. "Okay, a baggie with what appeared to be fragments of marijuana, a lighter, rolling papers. The roommate said the deceased had just 'scored a baggie' of marijuana and planned to smoke it that night to help him sleep."

Dr. Graves frowned. *Marijuana use is usually pretty low-key.*

Could cause some paranoia in some people—his thoughts were cut off by Kat's gasp.

"This is..." Kat frowned. "You haven't, uhh, looked at the scene photos yet, have you?"

"Not yet. Why?" He stepped toward her but she swiveled the screen away from his gaze. "What?"

She laid a hand on his cheek. "Just, well, it's—" She huffed out a frustrated breath. "There's a lot of blood, and, and I know *I* haven't seen this kind of scene since..."

Now he understood why she looked worried, and pale. He nodded. "No need to say it. Perhaps I shouldn't look at the photos until after I'm done here—just in case."

The crease between Kat's eyebrows relaxed, and she moved her hand back to the mouse, probably closing out of the photo attachment.

Dr. Graves took a steadying breath and forced thoughts of bloody crime scenes out of his head. "I'm going to record now."

After clicking on the microphone, he began his dictation. "Nineteen-year-old male, appears to have been in good physical condition. The deceased is wearing boxer-briefs. Dried blood coats the boxers and much of his lower body, lower limbs, and bilateral hands—with a larger amount of blood on the right hand and halfway up the right forearm." Dr. Graves moved closer to the deceased's right hand. "The deceased has a large ring on his right fourth finger," with gloved hands, Dr. Graves picked up the victim's arm to closer examine the ring, "it appears to be a class ring with a large stone. The ring is turned so the stone is facing outward from the palm side of the hand." He adjusted the light to shine directly on the ring. "Bits of flesh are observed clinging to the prongs of the ring."

He turned the mic off and inspected the boxers before cutting them off. "Kat, take a picture of this, please." He held the boy's leg at an angle so Kat could take a photo of a tear in the material at the inner thigh. "Label that photo 'tear, boxers, right inner thigh'."

Kat wrote it down in the first line of the photo list.

Since the boxers were still moist with the blood, Dr. Graves laid them out on a sterile drape to dry before placing them in a paper evidence bag. He removed the ring and examined it closer before placing it in its own bag. "It's a class ring. A high school ring," he said, his voice low and solemn.

Kat and Dr. Graves worked together to clean the blood off the deceased before Dr. Graves continued with his dictation. "No lividity noted on the body, denoting a rapid loss of blood. The skin of the groin area and inner thighs is red and flaky with small bumps resembling a tinea cruris infection. There is a tear in the skin of the left groin area, eight centimeters in length, through all layers of skin and underlying tissue, jagged edges."

He paused the recording. "Well, now we know where he bled out from. We just need to figure out how it happened."

During the autopsy, Dr. Graves took samples of the liver and brain to send for toxicology screens since there wasn't enough blood in the deceased's system to send. "Besides the routine tox screen, put a note in there for the crime lab to run a screen for drugs commonly used to lace marijuana."

Kat nodded. While she prepared the tissue samples, Dr. Graves continued his dictation as he sewed the young man's chest and abdomen back together. "Autopsy revealed a near-total transection of the superficial femoral artery. Relative blood loss is estimated to be near one-hundred percent. Also noted was organ pallor and shock kidneys. The superior vena cava, main pulmonary artery, and right pulmonary artery were all collapsed. Cause of death is determined to be fatal hemorrhage from a torn femoral artery. Undetermined at this time if this was self-inflicted, accidental, or homicide."

They cleaned up in silence, Dr. Graves' mulling over his findings and the possible scenarios that could have caused this unfortunate death. He barely registered when the morgue phone rang and Kat answered. "Medical Examiner's office, Kat speaking."

Dr. Graves half listened to Kat's side of the conversation.

"Yes, we've just completed the autopsy... Yes, we can have

everything cleaned up in time for them to view the body... Okay. Thank you for the heads-up... Bye."

She didn't need to tell him what the call had been about. "The parents?" he asked, anyway.

Kat nodded and looked over at the cold drawer they'd just slid someone's son into. Someone's dead son. "They're coming from out of town. They'll be here in about two hours."

His jaw tightened. He hated this part. All the raw emotion, anger, grief, questions. Questions he didn't always have answers to this early in the process. Chief Billings always wanted him to be there, though, to answer what he could. "Let's grab a bite to eat, then get him ready for his parents to see him," he said quietly.

Kat nodded.

Neither of them had much of an appetite, but they both ate enough of their brought-from-home lunches to give them some stamina to get through the rest of the day.

They worked together to prepare the deceased. Kat took extra care to arrange his hair over the incisions in his scalp where they'd cut into his skull to get to his brain. There was no way to make the cold table or the colder atmosphere of the morgue more pleasant, so Dr. Graves had long ago started purchasing a variety of quilts to tuck around the bodies in these situations, so at least the loved-ones weren't facing a corpse draped in a cold, white sheet. He picked one that matched the colors of the college the young man had been attending, tucking it around him and making sure none of the incisions he'd made were visible. At the last minute, he uncovered one of the boy's hands. Moms always needed a hand to hold.

SIXTEEN

Dr. Graves' mood was still solemn as time for the meeting with the scientist rolled around. The scene the day before with the college boy's parents had been hard. It was difficult enough to watch a mom mourn the death of her son, but when the dad broke down into spine-breaking sobs, Dean had to excuse himself. The walls of his office weren't thick enough to drown out the heart wrenching sounds. And the conclusion he'd mostly come to regarding how this unlikely death occurred, wasn't one he could share yet, not until the tox report came back.

Kat drove to the Starbucks Andrew Matheson had indicated for the meeting. Dean was thankful she didn't ask him if he was okay. How do you answer that so shortly after witnessing such grief? She just laid her hand on his while she drove and let him brood in silence.

Although they arrived five minutes early—because if you aren't five minutes early you're late—the scientist beat them there. Dr. Graves knew immediately which patron he was. He had a disheveled, yet intelligent, look Dr. Graves recognized from looking in the mirror.

The man stood a few inches shorter than him. He kept his hands firmly in his pockets, which Dr. Graves appreciated as someone averse to shaking hands.

The man nodded. "Dr. Graves, it's a pleasure to meet you. I'm Andrew Matheson." He looked at Kat and smiled without showing any teeth. "And you brought your assistant, I see."

"Yes, Dr. Matheson. This is Katherine. It's nice to meet you as well."

Kat smiled. "Why don't you two get started while I go grab Dr. Graves and me a drink."

"Thanks, Kat," Dr. Graves said. He sat across from Andrew and started right in. "So Dr. Matheson, what are your thoughts on this outbreak?"

"Please, call me Andrew. Before I share my thoughts with you, is there anything else about the case I should know other than what has been on the news?"

Dr. Graves had to tread lightly with information. There were certain things the investigators in Atlanta and Augusta wanted to keep from public knowledge during this phase of the investigation. "Not really, for once the news got it mostly right. This strain is unlike any other known strain of *Legionella*, with the same four serogroups being isolated from every case. The CDC does not think this is something that could have come about naturally. And I agree with them."

Andrew nodded, forehead creased. "Yes. Definitely sounds manmade. What do you think about the showerhead theory the news is touting?"

"It seems to be a common factor in some of the cases."

Andrew raised an eyebrow. "I don't see how, exactly. I would think there would be more clusters of cases if the showerheads were the contaminate. But, of course, I'm not privy to everything that you know."

Exactly what he'd thought. How much information should he trust this man with? Dr Graves turned in his seat to look for Kat. She was so much better at reading people than he was. He was surprised at the relief he felt when he spotted her walking toward them with two cups of coffee and some bagels in her hands. "It's a fairly new theory," Dr. Graves said as he turned back to the scientist. "Questions are still being asked and tests are still being run. But I agree, there has to be more to it."

Kat sat next to him and placed a cup and a bagel in front of him.

"Thanks, Kat." He smiled at her and turned back in time to see

Andrew looking at them with a spark of discovery in his eyes and a wry smile on his lips. Dr. Graves did not like it. The look made his stomach churn.

"So," Kat said. "Have you two solved this mystery yet?"

Andrew laughed. "We may be geniuses, Dr. Graves and I, but even great men such as us need a little longer than a few minutes to solve this one."

Kat smiled. "Oh, I don't believe that. I think you were just waiting for me to get back to the table so you'd have an audience for your greatness."

The crease between Dean's eyebrows deepened. Was she *flirting* with this man? She grasped his hand under the table and squeezed. No. No, of course she wasn't. He concentrated on relaxing his facial muscles. "I just finished filling Dr. Matheson in on what we know. And he was about to tell me what he thinks." Dr. Graves gestured to the scientist.

Andrew opened his mouth to speak, but Kat cut him off. "Sorry to interrupt, but I'm curious as to your background," she said. "Would you mind telling us a little about yourself?"

Smart. Dr. Graves gave her hand a squeeze.

"Yes, of course." The scientist sat back and took a sip of his coffee, eyeing Kat with an appreciative gaze over the cup. "As I said in my email communication, I graduated from Harvard with a master's degree, and, to the great disappointment of the entire microbiology department there, I chose to receive my PhD from Oxford."

"Oh?" Kat tilted her head. "Why is that?"

"I was ready for a change of scenery."

Kat laughed. "I've never been to England, but I can't imagine it's that much different from Massachusetts. Except the accents, of course."

This time his smile was full-toothed and aimed only at Kat. "You are correct, my dear. It was mundanely similar. I should have gone to Singapore or Brazil, but then I would have had to take the time to learn a new language, and the seven I already speak seemed enough at the time."

Kat's eyes widened. "You speak *seven* languages?"

Dr. Graves stopped himself from rolling his eyes and cleared his throat. "While that is fascinating and impressive, I'm more interested in your time with the CDC."

The scientist's eyes turned cold and his nostrils flared. But only for a brief moment before he nodded to Dr. Graves with a closed-mouth smile. "I don't believe I mentioned that in my email, Dr. Graves."

"No, you didn't. But a quick internet search brought it up. I'm sure you understand my wanting to validate your credentials before agreeing to meet with you."

"Yes, of course." A small muscle in his jaw twitched. "And, may I ask, what did you find out about my time there? I don't want to bore you with information you already have knowledge of."

"Only that you were hired as the assistant lead microbiologist, I figured I could get the rest from you."

The muscles in Dr. Matheson's face relaxed. "Yes, well, I worked there for five years before deciding on a new path. I felt that my genius could be used for nobler endeavors. I believe that science should be used to help advance mankind toward a stronger future."

Kat spread cream cheese on her bagel and, without looking up from the task, asked, "And what have you been doing since then? I'd love to hear about some of the ways you've helped mankind."

"I've been doing whatever I want," he replied with a laugh. "But really, I have been traveling, guest lecturing at universities around the world. I've also been continuing my own research—which is really where my contribution to the betterment of the human race lies."

"Where?" Dr. Graves asked. His search on the web hadn't shown any positions Matheson had held since the CDC.

Andrew's eyes pivoted to him. "I have my own, well-equipped lab in my home." He laughed again and grinned. "Try not to look so alarmed, Dr. Graves. It isn't as 'evil-scientist' as it sounds. I am obviously not licensed, as an individual, to obtain or work with dangerous substances. I mostly find ways to help small companies improve their products or family farms to improve their crops using organic methods. Things like that."

Dr. Graves relaxed a little. He was being too paranoid.

"That sounds amazing," Kat said. "What a great use of your scientific genius."

"Thank you, Katherine," Dr. Matheson said. "I do feel like I should try to improve the world while I'm in it."

Dean wasn't sure why this exchange annoyed him, but it did. "Let's get back to why we're here, Kat and I will need to be getting back to work soon. Do you have any thoughts about the *Legionella* Tetrad epidemic that we haven't already looked into?"

"Is there anything specific you would like my input on?" he asked.

"Two things. First and foremost, treatment. The ICU and Infectious Disease doctors aren't having a lot of luck with what they've tried. So far, this bacteria has a 100% kill rate. And second, as we briefly touched on already, it's been bothering me as to how this thing works—any thoughts on why it seems to only be infecting one person per location? Or, per showerhead if that ends up being the vector?"

The scientist thought for a moment, tapping his fingers on the table as he stared down at them. He drew in a breath and looked up at Dr. Graves. "I have some ideas—some very solid ideas from things I worked on at the CDC. But I would need to run a few tests to be sure. I need to see how this tetrad of *Legionella* serogroups reacts to different methods of delivery." He looked from Dean to Kat. "Would you be able to get me a sample?"

Dr. Graves' first instinct was to shout a vehement "no!" He tamped that instinct down, though. What had he expected the scientist to do? Of course he would need a sample to work with, how else would he be able to run tests on it? He swallowed. "I'll have to get permission from the health department and law enforcement. What kinds of samples are you thinking?"

Dr. Matheson nodded. "Of course. Ideally I would need both a water sample from a known source of infection and a blood sample from a patient with an active case." He looked down, tapping his fingers again. "You, uhh, you don't need to get permission from the CDC?"

"I hadn't thought of that. I don't believe I'll need to." Dr. Graves narrowed his eyes at Andrew. "Why does that seem to make you nervous, Dr. Matheson?"

"Oh." He sat up straight and smiled. "It does not make me nervous. There is just some, let's say, *bad blood* there. They were not happy to be losing a brain such as mine, and things turned... unpleasant...when I refused their multiple offers." He shook his head. "Like a stalker who just cannot take no for an answer."

Dr. Graves would definitely be contacting the CDC, but Dr. Matheson didn't need to know that. "I'll work on getting the permissions I need. The water sample shouldn't be a problem, but we might have to content ourselves with that. Getting permission to obtain a blood sample might not be possible."

"I understand, but please do try. I am confident I can find an effective treatment."

Gathering his empty coffee cup and bagel, Dr. Graves stood. "I'll contact you on Monday, Dr. Matheson, to let you know where we stand. Thank you for reaching out to me."

"You are welcome. I look forward to working on this with you."

—⋀—

DEAN STARED out the passenger window on the drive back to the morgue, sorting through his mixed thoughts and emotions. Was he jealous? Was that the sentiment tugging at his chest? It had seemed as though Kat had been flirting with Dr. Matheson. He turned to her as she drove. "What are your thoughts about Andrew Matheson?"

"I think he has a very high opinion of himself, and perhaps that is deserved. I mean, he seems smart enough."

"Like a 'scientific genius'?" He used her own words, realizing as he said them that it really did bother him.

Kat glanced at him and smiled, that mischievous sparkle he loved so much dancing in her eyes. "Why, Dean Graves, if I didn't know any better, I'd think you're jealous."

Face flushing, Dean cleared his throat. She wasn't wrong. "Maybe a little."

She laughed. "Well, there's no need for you to be. I detected Dr. Matheson's need for praise right away and figured it to be the best way to ply him for information. Sometimes flirting and compliments can be used as nothing more than a tool, Dean. And there's only room for one genius in my life, and that is you." She pressed her warm hand against his cheek.

And her touch calmed his inner turmoil, even though she only had one hand on the steering wheel.

SEVENTEEN

"I'm pretty sure this is the tree." Dean stood gazing up into the thin branches of the tree Hermione had scared the orange cat up the two days ago. The pathway beneath the trees didn't seem quite as fearsome with the mid-day sunlight streaming through breaks in the leafy canopy.

"Well, she appears to have made it back down on her own." Kat stood close to him, scanning the area for signs of the cat.

"I hope so." He turned a worried face to Kat. "You don't think she fell and hurt herself, do you? Maybe we should look around a little more."

Kat snuggled in to his side and smiled wryly up at him. "Why, Dr. Graves, if I didn't know any better, I'd think you were trying to lure me into the forest so you can have your way with me."

He knew she was joking with him and decided to prove how much he'd changed by playing along. He cocked an eyebrow at her and whispered, "And would that be such a bad thing, Miss Flanagan?"

"Definitely not," she whispered back before raising up on her toes to kiss his cheek. She grabbed his free hand, the other held onto Hermione's leash, and pulled him into the cover of the trees. "Come on, doctor, let's go see if we can find that cat you're worried about."

The playful grin on her face pushed all thoughts of the little creature from his mind. There was only one Kat he was interested in at the moment. He pulled her to a stop a few yards in where they couldn't see the trail and a group of trees made a perfect little hideaway with their overlapping branches. Dean looped the leash around a low bush and told Hermione to sit, then turned to Kat.

He gripped her waist and pulled her close. Her arms wrapped around his neck as their lips met and her body melted into his, fitting together like two halves of the same whole. He forgot about everything in that moment. His world was Kat. The fresh scent of her shampoo, the softness of her lips, the curiosity of her tongue gently probing his, the warmth of her body pressed to his, the taste of lingering mint on her breath. He slipped his hands under her t-shirt, caressing the soft skin of her back. She curled her fingers in his hair, increasing the pressure of the kiss, encouraging his roaming hands with a quiet moan.

Heart pounding out a rapid rhythm in his chest, Dean moved his hands to Kat's sides, his thumbs resting just below her bra-line.

Rustling branches, a loud bark, and a yowl broke the trance. Dean pulled away from the single greatest kiss of his life, removing his hands from inside Kat's shirt as he growled, "Damnit. Hermione get back here!"

"Looks like she found your stray cat." Kat's flushed cheeks and increased respirations made his legs turn to jelly.

"Damnit," he whispered again with a shake of his head. "I'd already found my Kat."

"And you aren't going to lose her. Ever." Her voice shook just a little.

He stepped toward her, ready to resume what had been interrupted. Hermione's bark came to them from a distance. For the third time in less than half a minute Dean swore.

"We'd better go find her," Kat said, placing a hand on his chest.

"Yeah," he sighed.

⌁

DEAN COULD ONLY BE ANNOYED with Hermione for a few seconds after she ran back to him on the path, her tail wagging proudly. The cat was nowhere to be seen. Dean patted the dog's head and bent to grab her leash, whispering to her loud enough for Kat to hear, "You have very bad timing when I'm not having nightmares, girl."

The dog licked his face, still wagging her tail in excitement.

They walked back to Dean's house hand-in-hand. He kept stealing glances at Kat as his thoughts returned again and again to the kiss they'd just shared. It was by far the most passionate one yet—and the warmth and joy pumping through his body with each beat of his pounding heart was evidence that he was ready for more. But he didn't want to bring it up now. Not when there was a chance someone could hear them talking. Heat rushed to his face at the thought.

"What do you think about Dr. Matheson's request for samples?" Dean asked, though his mind was far from the subject he'd chosen to pass the time before they were safely alone in his house.

Kat shrugged. "I don't see how it could hurt. He seems to be legitimately smart. Full of himself, but smart. I think he might be able to help if by nothing more than to bring a new perspective to the case. Maybe he can think of something the rest of you haven't thought of simply because he's coming at it from a different angle."

"I had those same thoughts, and I hope that's the case."

"But?"

Dean shook his head. "I don't know. I just...something just feels off. You're better at reading people than I am. Did you get any feelings that something isn't right?"

Kat shrugged. "Maybe. I mean, he's odd, that's for sure. That's why I was trying to encourage him to talk about himself, to see if there were any inconsistencies. Part of me wonders if he's just a stuffed shirt, wanting to somehow prove himself to be smarter than the people he worked with at the CDC. Was there something specific that bothered you?"

"Yes. Speaking of the CDC, he seemed a little worried when he asked if I'd have to talk to them about getting him a sample."

Nodding slowly, Kat agreed, "Yeah, he did."

"Which means I need to talk to someone from the CDC to see why he really parted ways with them."

"That's a good idea. But maybe he just doesn't like the idea of someone snooping into his past. He acted a little put-off that you even searched his name, like his privacy is important to him."

"I can understand that. But I'll give the CDC a call on Monday anyway, just in case." They'd reached Dean's house and his stomach erupted with the proverbial butterfly sensations as he thought about what he wanted to say to Kat before he talked himself out of it.

As he unclipped the leash from Hermione's collar and hung it on the hook by the door, he thought about how to bring up the subject of...of moving forward in their relationship. Specifically in the physical part of their relationship. He huffed, irritated with himself for feeling like a teenager in this situation.

"Everything okay?" Kat asked.

He breathed deeply and held it in for a few seconds. "Yes. Yes, everything is fine. Let's sit down. There's something I want to talk to you about."

Kat's face fell, worry taking over the shine that had been in her eyes just moments ago. "Okay."

Dean was doing this all wrong. He smiled and took her hand, leading her over to the couch. "Don't look so worried. This is one of those good talks. I think. I mean, I hope you feel that way too."

They sat side by side, legs touching. Dean's heart vaulted itself against his sternum repeatedly. Needing to change the mood between them, he gave in to his instincts and caressed her face, tucking her hair behind her ear. Keeping his eyes locked with hers, he leaned in and touched his lips to hers. Gently at first, eyes now closed, until the heat that had overtaken him, them, in the forest rushed through his body again. Holding her face between his hands, he ended the kiss and laid his forehead against hers. After giving himself a few seconds to recover his voice, he leaned back, reached for her hand and brought it to his chest, and said, more sure now than ever, "Kat, I love you so much. In the trees, when we kissed, I... It felt amazing. You felt amazing." *Just say it, Dean*, he chastised himself. "Kat, I'm ready to...to move to the next level in our relationship. If you are, I mean."

Kat's breath rushed out in a relieved sigh. She smiled, then laughed. "If by 'the next level' you mean making love, I've been ready since the night you first kissed me, Dean."

Leave it to Kat to get right to the point when he could only dance around it in uncomfortable stutters. He returned her smile and squeezed her hand he had pressed to his chest. "Yes, Katherine Flanagan, that is exactly what I mean. But not because of the feelings your touch stirs in me—well, not *only* because of that—but because everything about us is right. I can't imagine not having you in my life. You are the first thing I think of when I wake up in the morning, and the last thing I think of before I go to sleep at night. You're the one I want to tell everything to: the good, the bad, the mundane." He looked down and chuckled before returning his gaze to her now moist eyes. "Not to ruin the moment by bringing my mom up, but I finally understand why it was important to her that I wait. Why she taught me to respect women, and that part of that respect was to *know* before jumping into bed with a woman. To know who she is, to know I love her, to know I never want to live without her, to know she knows me and accepts who I am and loves me anyway. The knowing comes first because the act is an emotional and physical bond. And it's important. It isn't something trivial to be given away to just anyone."

"Oh, Dean." Kat's voice quivered. "Your mom was right. I wish I would have been given that same advice when I was younger. I am so grateful to that wonderful woman for raising the man I love."

"I wish she could have met you. She would love you. She would approve." He smiled and pulled Kat into a hug.

They sat in the silent embrace for several minutes. Dean kissed the top of her head and said, "I want our first time to be special. We've waited this long, are you okay to wait just a little longer so I can make some arrangements?"

"I am okay to wait, Dean, but you don't need to do anything special."

"I want to. Next weekend. We'll go away somewhere." He paused then asked, "Will that work with your cycle?"

Kat burst into laughter. "Only Dean Graves would ask that like it was a perfectly normal question."

"Isn't it a normal question?" He leaned back to look at her.

Still laughing, she said, "I guess it should be, but I don't know another man who would even think to ask. But lucky for me, you aren't just any man. You are Dr. Dean Graves. You are *my* man."

EIGHTEEN

The loud, obnoxious buzzer sounded, signaling that someone without access was outside the morgue requesting entrance, jolting Dr. Graves back to reality Monday morning as he searched the internet for just the right weekend getaway for him and Kat. He couldn't remember the last time someone used the buzzer. Everyone who had a need to visit the morgue, had access. He shut down his browser, guilt at using his work computer for a non-work function getting the better of him. He pushed away from the desk to stand when Kat walked past from her office, pausing in his doorway long enough to smile and say, "I'll go see who it is."

Dr. Graves logged into his email to see that four of the five *Legionella* cases from the gym had succumbed to their infections. They were no longer requesting autopsies on these patients, there was no need, they knew what had killed them. He opened an email from the crime lab and was surprised to see toxicology results from the college kid's autopsy already. The new lab director had promised faster results, and so far she'd delivered. The results showed what Dr. Graves had suspected. He stood, he wanted to run it past Kat.

As he stepped into the hallway, intending to turn right to go to Kat's office, he heard muffled voices coming from the autopsy suite and remembered that someone had pushed the door buzzer. He turned left, heading toward the voices. "Kat?" he said as he entered the morgue.

"Oh, Dr. Graves, we were just about to come to your office." Kat leaned against the large sink casually, Andrew Matheson facing her from a few steps away.

Upon seeing the scientist, Dr. Graves remembered he'd planned to call his contact at the CDC to try to find out more about the man. "Dr. Matheson, what a surprise. What brings you here so early on a Monday morning?"

Dr. Matheson nodded at him. "Dr. Graves, good morning. I was just telling Katherine here that I had some ideas over the weekend. That isn't why I stopped by, though, not completely. I heard on the morning news that four more victims had died, and I'm just hoping I can do something to prevent further deaths."

"That is what we're all hoping to do."

"Yes, of course," Andrew said earnestly. "I'm afraid I can't do much without those samples I asked you about, though. I've designed some tests and have everything set up in my lab just waiting for the samples. Have you heard back from the police or health department?"

In fact, he had heard back and had planned to email the scientist shortly. "Why don't we go to my office." He didn't wait for a response, he just turned and led the way.

Once they were all situated around his desk, Dr. Graves said, "It looks like I'll be able to get you a small sample of the water that was flushed through one of the unused showerheads. Other than that, I'm afraid it's a no on the blood sample request."

"Oh, well, that's something I guess." The scientist frowned, disappointment evident on his face. "I'll have to do what I can with what I'm allowed. Do you have the sample here?"

"No, I'll have to submit some paperwork and then go to the lab and sign for it. I'm afraid I won't have time to get over there today." He really didn't have time, he had a follow-up appointment with the orthopedic doctor to check on how his hand had healed. But he also wanted to get some answers from the CDC before trusting this man.

"Okay," Dr. Matheson said. "I understand that you are busy. I just thought you might be anxious to have another great mind working on this, what with the recent rise in the death toll." He stood. "I'll wait for you to contact me, then."

"Thank you for your willingness to help," Dr. Graves said through a partially clenched jaw. "I should have a sample for you sometime tomorrow."

"I'll walk you out, Dr. Matheson," Kat said.

Dr. Graves tapped a pencil on his desk as he made a mental list of things he needed to get done. He started with an email to his contact at the CDC asking about the self-proclaimed genius who'd just left his office.

Kat returned several minutes later. He'd sent the email and filled out the request form to retrieve the water sample from the state lab before she came back into his office.

"Do you think you can stop by the lab and pick up that sample this afternoon? I have a doctor's appointment." He lifted his hand in explanation.

"Sure. Any special requirements?"

"You'll need to take the cooler to transport it in, it needs to stay refrigerated. You can just bring it back here and put it in the specimen fridge. I'll figure out how to get it to Dr. Matheson tomorrow."

Kat nodded.

"Oh, and I got the tox report back on that college student."

"And?"

"It appears that the marijuana he smoked was laced with phenylcyclohexyl piperidine—PCP."

"I didn't know that was even around anymore," Kat said. "Do you think that had something to do with his death?"

Dr. Graves nodded grimly. "I think it had everything to do with his death."

"How?"

"The evidence points to a scenario something like this: it starts with a bad case of tinea cruris, or jock itch—remember the flaming rash on his groin and upper thighs? He smokes the PCP-laced marijuana, who knows whether he realizes it's laced or not? My guess is not. His heart rate and blood pressure increase, he starts hallucinating, the itch becomes unbearable, and in the hallucinatory, hypersensitive state he's in, he scratches with great intensity. At some point his class ring twists on his finger so the large gem is on the palm side of his hand, it digs into his skin, ripping it, eventually severing his femoral artery as he continues to dig at the itching rash, oblivious of the pain or bleeding."

Kat's mouth hung open. "That's...that's just...terrible."

Dean nodded. "I'm going to give Detective Rodriguez a call. They may want to pursue homicide charges against whoever sold him the drugs."

⁓

GLANCING at the clock on his microwave, Dean hung his keys on the hook by the door. "It's a little early for dinner, girl," he said to Hermione.

He sent a text to Kat: *Got done early at doctor's. How did it go at the lab?*

Her return text popped up almost immediately: *Driving.* Kat had her phone set to automatically send that message when she was in the act of driving.

The temperature outside was too hot and humid to enjoy sitting on his porch at this time of day. Hermione had gone straight to her doggy bed when she realized he wasn't going to feed her yet. She must have played hard with Winston while Dean was at work. It was time to make the final arrangements for his weekend away with Kat. He smiled, and his heart skipped a beat at the thought. He grabbed his rarely used laptop and sat at the kitchen island to look up a small cottage on Sapelo Island he'd found earlier. At first he'd passed on it, as it was a three-hour drive plus a twenty-minute ferry ride to get to the island. But he decided on his way home that a three-hour road trip with Kat couldn't be anything but wonderful. And the secluded area where the cottage resided, plus miles of uninhabited beaches, was too great an opportunity to pass up.

After taking a deep breath, Dean clicked on the tab to book it. His fingers shook a little as he retrieved his credit card from his wallet and typed the numbers in. He leaned back, shoulders relaxed, and smiled when a screen popped up showing that the reservation was complete. He was really doing this. *They* were really going to do this. And he didn't think he'd ever been happier or more sure about a decision in his life.

He reached for his phone to text Kat, but Hermione, awake after her power-nap, nudged him and whined. Dean looked at the clock again. "I guess it's close enough," he said to the dog. "Let's get you some dinner." He measured out the proper amount of the dry dogfood recommended by the veterinarian and dumped it in Hermione's dish. His own stomach growled as he watched his dog devour her meal.

Thinking about dinner, he turned to get his phone. Maybe he would grill some hamburgers for him and Kat. The phone buzzed on the counter just before his hand reached it. He grinned like a school boy when he saw that it was Kat. "Hello, I was just—"

"Dean!" The panic in her voice slammed into him like a three-hundred-pound linebacker.

"Kat. What's wrong?" He gripped his phone so tight it hurt.

"I...I don't know what to do. I"—her voice cracked, and she took several shallow breaths—"I think I might have just been exposed to the, the tetrad."

Bile shot into Dean's throat as his stomach constricted. His vision wavered, and he grabbed onto the countertop to steady himself. "Where are you?"

"I'm driving." Her rapid breathing flooded his ears.

Dean composed himself. She needed him to be composed. "Kat, take some slow, deep breaths and pull over as soon as it's safe to do so."

Her shaky respirations calmed after a few breaths. The *click-click* of her blinker let Dean know she was pulling over.

"I'm sorry, Dean. I shouldn't have panicked. I've pulled over."

"Where are you? I'll come get you." He snatched his keys and opened the door to the garage. Hermione rushed over, wagging her tail and looking up at him expectantly. Dean patted her head and whispered, "Sorry, girl. You can't come."

"I'm not sure. I'll share my location from my phone."

Dean smacked his head in his hurry to get in the car. His phone buzzed with Kat's location. She was only eleven minutes away. His tires squealed as he took off down the street, determined to cut that time in half.

—∿—

"What about my car?" Kat asked as she buckled herself into his passenger seat.

"We'll worry about that later." He turned his worried gaze to her. "Kat, what happened?"

Tears welled up in her eyes and she looked down at her hands, clenched tight in her lap. "Andrew emailed me after you left for your appointment. He asked if I could bring the sample to him today because he'd just worked out a formula or something. I didn't think anything of it." She looked up at Dean and a tremor shook her body.

Pain lanced through his skull as he ground his teeth. He laid his hand on Kat's bouncing leg and forced softness into his voice. "What did he do?"

"It was fine at first. I handed him the cooler with the sample in it, and he asked if I wanted to see his lab. It was downstairs, no windows but lots of artificial lighting, fans, hoods, a big refrigerator/freezer." She wiped her face with the back of her hand and stared out the window for a few seconds before continuing. "He showed me a stack of petri dishes and started to explain his 'research' to me. I was just kind of wandering around, looking at things as he talked, and I noticed a detailed schematic of a showerhead on top of a messy desk."

Dean tensed. "Showerhead?"

Kat nodded and twisted in her seat to face him. The car swayed when a semi passed them as they sat parked on the shoulder of the road. "He hurried over and stood between me and the desk." She looked down and mumbled, "I was stupid. I should have acted like I hadn't seen it, but I just blurted out, 'why do you have that diagram'?"

Wiping a tear from her cheek, Dean said, "You are not stupid. I would have done the same thing."

"No. You wouldn't. I should have at least waited until I was closer to the door."

"What did he say?"

"He tried to explain it was research to help us, that he'd printed it from the internet just the other day. But it was older than a few days. It had writing in different colors of ink, torn around the edges.

"As he was talking, he moved over to a table in the center of the room, blocking me from the exit." She swiped at a stray hair in her face. "And, Dean, I just kept going. I was thinking about the deaths and the families. I asked him what really happened at the CDC and where he got all the equipment for his home lab."

Dean held her hand and waited for her to finish.

"He changed then. Briefly. His face contorted, and he said, 'the CDC is nothing but a bunch of bumbling idiots.' Then he seemed to gain control of himself. I told him I needed to leave, and he stepped out of the way..." The tears spilled in torrents down her face now. "But when I rushed past him he pulled a tube from a...a machine thing and sprayed it in my face—just as I inhaled."

Anger raged through Dean's veins. He let go of Kat's hand, afraid he might break it as the uncontrolled fury hit him with the force of an atom bomb. He curled his hand into a tight fist, the pinch of pain from the recent fracture somehow stopping him from driving his fist into the steering wheel.

"Dean." Somehow, his whispered name on Kat's lips broke through. "What am I going to do?"

Dean put his car in gear and looked before pulling out onto the road, spraying gravel far into the trees lining the shoulder. "Hey Siri!"

He was surprised the AI recognized the growl that had become his voice. "Call Chief Billings."

The Chief of Police answered, "Hey, Dean, what's up?"

"Meet me at the U hospital. I'll be there in ten minutes. ER."

"What—?"

"I'll explain there." Dean stabbed at the 'end call' button.

NINETEEN

"Dr. Graves." The ER doctor stood with his arms crossed outside the curtained room the triage nurse had taken Kat to. "What do you expect us to do? She doesn't have any symptoms. You can't know for sure what she was sprayed with..."

"I'll tell you *exactly* what I want you to do, that way, you won't have to think for yourselves." Dr. Graves looked away from the exasperating man and pinched the bridge of his nose, trying to tamp down the anger and panic arising from his fear for Kat. He looked back at the doctor. "Call Dr. Shah to admit her to the hospital, I'll talk to him if you want. Start an IV and give her levofloxacin, rifampin, and azithromycin—you can think of it as prophylactic treatment if it makes you feel better, like you would do for someone with a potential exposure to HIV or meningitis." Dean leaned in closer to the doctor. "And you will *stop* telling me to take her home and come back when she develops symptoms."

The ER doctor puffed up his chest, his face red. "Look, I don't try to tell you how to do your autopsies, so don't come into my ER and try to tell me what to do."

Dean stepped toward him and the man stumbled back a couple of steps.

"Jill, call security," the doctor yelled over his shoulder at the clerk.

"No need for that." Chief Tracey Billings, accompanied by a nurse, walked toward the two doctors.

Relaxing his stance a fraction, Dean continued to glare at the stubborn ER doctor.

When Tracey reached them, she glanced at the nametag clipped to the ER doctor's lab coat. "Dr. Jasper, give Dr. Graves and me a moment, please."

Dr. Jasper looked from the badge and nametag on Tracey's uniform to Dean then to Tracey. With a stiff nod, he spun and hurried away.

"Dean, what the hell is going on?"

He gestured to the curtained room. "Let's go in here so Kat can explain." Dean rubbed his temples, a pounding headache beating against the inside of his skull.

About two sentences into Kat's account, Tracey stopped her to pull a small notebook out of a pocket in her duty belt. "Continue." She looked at Kat and clicked her pen.

Tracey didn't interrupt again until Kat got to the part about him spraying the unknown substance in her face. "Did he say anything to you?"

"He said 'oops, sorry. Don't worry, it's nothing dangerous.' Then he followed me upstairs and to his front door."

"What's his address?"

Kat pointed to the countertop where her purse sat. "Hand me my phone, Dean, it's in there."

He handed her the purse, uncomfortable with the thought of searching through it to find her phone.

Hands shaking, Kat pulled her phone out of a side pocket and opened the map. She handed the phone to Chief Billings as a nurse came in carrying an IV insertion tray.

Tracey clicked the button on her radio and tilted her head toward the mic clipped to the shoulder of her uniform, speaking into it. "Dispatch this is Chief Billings."

A female voice surrounded by mild static replied, "Go ahead, chief."

"Send backup, 10-40, to"—she glanced at Kat's phone—"the residence at 1257 Oak Street. I will meet them there with detectives. Instruct them to wait for my arrival."

"10-4, chief."

"What's 10-40?" Dean asked.

"No lights or sirens." Tracey stepped to Kat's bedside and her voice softened as she said, "We'll get him. And your boss, here, will make sure you get the best available care." To Dean she said, "I'll keep you informed, and I expect that you'll do likewise."

"Thank you, Tracey. I will."

The chief had her phone to her ear before she even stepped out of the room. "Fitzpatrick, you and Davis meet me at..." her voice faded as she hurried to the exit.

The nurse, who had been standing just inside the door since entering the room, set the IV tray on a metal stand and pushed it up to the head of the bed. She glanced at Dean with a nervous smile then looked back down at Kat as she lowered the side rail then scooted the exam stool over to sit on. "Dr. Shah is going to admit you to the medical floor. He should be coming to talk to you in fifteen or twenty minutes. I'm going to insert an IV so I can get the first round of antibiotics started."

"Thank God." Dean collapsed into a chair, the exhaustion of holding every muscle taut in fear and frustration for the past hour finally affecting him.

As the nurse inserted the IV catheter into Kat's arm and filled several tubes with blood, she said, "Dr. Shah agreed with your plan, Dr. Graves." In a hushed tone she added, "And Dr. Jasper wasn't at all happy with me for paging him behind his back."

Kat reached over with her free hand as the nurse put the last piece of tape over the IV site and touched her arm. "Thank you, Katie. I hope you don't get too much flack for doing that."

She shrugged. "I'm not too worried about it. It's my job to be a patient advocate." She stood and raised the side rail back up. "The orders should be in the computer by now so I'll go get the first antibiotic ready. I'll be back shortly."

"Thank you," Dr. Graves said. He pulled the chair over to the bed and took Kat's hand.

"I'm scared, Dean."

"I know. So am I." He didn't know if he should have admitted that, but he didn't have the mental or emotional stamina at the moment to figure it out. So he just resorted to the no-filters honesty he'd practiced his entire life. "But we've got a jump on this. And we're learning more about this bacteria every day. And hopefully the police can confiscate the equipment and substance he sprayed you with so we can see exactly what it is."

She squeezed his hand and sighed. "Someday you'll learn to just tell me everything's going to be okay."

He ran his free hand through his hair. A lump formed in his throat and he couldn't swallow, the pressure radiating up to his jaws and down to his chest. Finally he was able to force a whisper past the lump. "Everything is going to be okay, Kat." But it wasn't. How could it? They didn't know how to successfully treat this. It was killing people. It was killing everyone infected with it. He dropped his head into his hand and tugged at his hair.

"What room is Katherine Flanagan in?" Dr. Shah's sharp Indian accent carried into the room from the nurse's station. He entered through the curtains a moment later.

Dean tried to compose himself before he looked up. "Dr. Shah. Thank you."

He wagged his head back and forth. "Of course, Dean. I agree with your suggested antibiotic regimen, and I ordered some labs."

Dean stood and moved the chair so Dr. Shah could examine Kat.

"Katherine, as you probably already know, I am Dr. Shah. I am an infectious disease doctor and I, along with the hospitalist that's on today, Dr. Bingham, are going to admit you to the hospital. Katie told me what happened so I won't make you repeat everything to me, but I do have two questions. What time were you exposed to the aerosolized bacteria? And, how are you feeling?"

The background noise of the busy ER intruded on the small space of the silent room while Kat thought. She looked up at Dean with wide eyes. "I've lost track of the time. It happened maybe five minutes before I called you. What time was that?"

Dean pulled his phone out and looked at it. "That was about an hour and a half ago."

"Okay," Dr. Shah said. "And my second question: how are you feeling?"

She hesitated before speaking. "I'm probably just being paranoid..."

Laying a hand on her shoulder, Dr. Shah said, "It's very important that you tell me about any symptoms you may be having, even if you're worried they are psychosomatic."

"I know you well, Kat," Dean said. "We both know you aren't prone to hysterics. Tell us what you're feeling."

She closed her eyes and took a deep breath, releasing it between pursed lips. "I feel like I'm coming down with something—like the day before you're laid low with the full-on flu. And I feel like it's harder to breathe than it was just an hour ago."

"Can you sit up for me so I can listen to your lungs?" Dr. Shah took her arm and helped her sit. He placed his stethoscope on her right upper back. "Just breathe in and out slowly through your mouth."

Her chest rose and fell as she complied.

Moving to her left upper back, he said, "Again."

He continued side to side until reaching the bottom of her lungs. His brow furrowed, he removed the stethoscope from his ears and hung it around his neck. "I'm going to order a chest x-ray."

Dean's muscles all tightened at once. "What did you hear?"

"It is very subtle, but there is a decrease in breath sounds in the bases bilaterally."

The room curtain parted and Katie entered pushing a pole with an IV pump attached. A bag labeled "Azithromycin" hung above it with the connected tubing disappearing into the top of the pump and reappearing out the bottom.

"Katie," Dr. Shah said. "Can you please help Ms. Flanagan get a urine sample before starting that?"

"Sure." She lowered the side rail and helped Kat to the bathroom.

Dean slumped back into the chair. "If she's exhibiting symptoms already..."

Pulling the exam stool over, Dr. Shah sat next to him. "I'm going to be straight with you, Dean. If the bacteria is already infecting her lungs, we are most likely dealing with a more concentrated, stronger strain of the *Legionella* tetrad, or something altogether different."

TWENTY

By the time Kat was settled in a private room on the medical floor, receiving her first dose of antibiotic number three, the sun was just barely hanging on to the western horizon. Dean kissed her forehead, then her lips. "I just have to go take care of Hermione and grab a couple of things then I'll be back."

"You don't need to come back tonight, Dean. Just get some sleep and I'll see you tomorrow." Her damp, overly bright and wide eyes belied her words.

"Kat, don't." He lifted her hand to his mouth and kissed it. "I'll be back. Tonight. Soon."

The streetlamps flickered on as the last rays of the sun disappeared. Dean's thoughts flitted around in his head like fireflies on crack. He'd never left Hermione home alone and not in her kennel, what if she tore up his couch? He had to find a way to cure Kat. Did the police catch Andrew? Did they have a sample of what he sprayed her with? Could he use it to find a cure? Maybe he should find the scientist himself and use some of the things Carter Ridge taught him to get to the truth. He shook his head. No. He wouldn't let Ridge get back in his head.

The house was dark as he pulled into the garage. The sound of dog claws scratching at the door met his ears as he reached for the doorknob. Hermione whined and wiggled, blocking his way in. "Okay, girl. I'm sorry I left you alone, now get out of the way and let's see what damage you caused in your doggy anxiety."

Three pillows from the couch were on the floor, but other than that it looked like she'd controlled herself quite well. Dean let her out back to do her business while he stood on the patio, watching the stars appear in the darkening sky. He called Amy next door and asked if she could dog-sit for a few days. He'd really underestimated what a great neighbor she'd been all these years. She didn't pry into his business by asking him where he was going, she just said, "Sure, bring her over."

He gathered a few of Hermione's favorite toys and dumped some dog food into two gallon-sized zip bags. The reflection in his bathroom mirror stared back at him with hair sticking up all over and bags under his frightened eyes. He shoved a few necessities into an overnight bag and turned out the light without looking back at the unfamiliar face in the mirror.

His phone buzzed. Tracey. "Hello," Dean answered.

"I just wanted to keep you updated. Andrew Matheson appears to have skipped town, looks like we missed him by about fifteen minutes. We got a warrant and sent hazmat in. Looked like Matheson took a bunch of stuff with him but they were able to find a few samples—tubes, petri dishes, a laptop—from his lab."

"Where are the samples going?"

"We haven't determined that yet. Probably a split between the crime lab and the CDC."

"Send me a list of the items you took," he said, then added, "Please."

"Wanna wait until Fitzpatrick has it all typed up or do you just want me to send you a picture of his chicken-scratched notes?"

"Just send a picture. There isn't enough time to wait on anything."

"Will do."

"Thank you, Tracey."

"How's Kat?"

"Okay so far. They admitted her. I'm on my way back there now."

"Keep me posted. I'll check in with you tomorrow." Tracey ended the call.

Dean grabbed his laptop and overnight bag and put them in his car before taking Hermione to the neighbor's.

As Dean handed Hermione's leash, food, and toys to Amy, he said, "Thank you. If you ever need me to return the favor with Winston, just call."

"It's no problem, Dean. I hope everything is okay."

"I hope so too," he murmured.

—∧—

Sweat beaded on Kat's forehead, and she shivered under the sheet and blanket of the hospital bed. Dean dropped his bag on a chair and rushed to her, feeling her forehead like his mom used to do when he complained of not feeling well. "You're burning up! When was the last time they checked on you?"

She mumbled, "Can't remember."

The pulse oximeter beeped a steady rhythm overhead. Dean studied the numbers and had to grab the side rail to keep from losing his balance.

"What?" Kat stared up at him with glossy eyes.

He reached for the call light and pushed the button. "Your heart rate is high, probably because you have a fever, and your oxygen level is...lower than it should be."

She twisted around in the bed to look at the monitor. "Ninety isn't too bad, is it?"

"No, but it was ninety-six in the ER less than two hours ago."

A nurse in black scrubs came in the room. "Can I help you?"

"She has a fever, her heart rate is high, and her oxygen is dropping."

The nurse replied in what was probably supposed to be a soothing tone, "It's normal for the heart rate to go up with a fever, though she didn't have a fever when I checked on admission. And as long as her oxygen stays above ninety, that's good."

Dean closed his eyes in a slow blink as he tried not to explode.

The nurse hadn't said anything that wasn't true. But she also didn't understand the severity of the situation. "Let me start over. I'm Dr. Dean Graves. I know what normal, or at least acceptable, vital signs are. I'm worried because she is getting worse at a rapid pace. As you said, she didn't have a fever the last time you checked. Her oxygen saturation was ninety-six in the ER—that's a big drop to ninety." He rubbed his temples. "Could you please check her temperature and blood pressure, give her an antipyretic, and let Dr. Shah and the hospitalist know about the change in her vital signs."

"Oh, okay. Yes, let me go get the blood pressure machine."

By the time she returned less than a minute later, the pulse oximeter was alarming with a high-pitched tone. Her oxygen level had dropped to eighty-eight percent.

The nurse took her temperature and frowned. "It's 104.2."

Kat's blood pressure was 102/59.

The nurse ripped open a nasal cannula package and hooked it up to the oxygen regulator on the wall. She turned the oxygen on at four liters per minute and put the cannula prongs in Kat's nose, wrapping the tubing around her ears and tightening it under her chin to keep it in place. "I'm going to go page the doctors now." She hurried out, a little paler than she'd been when she'd first answered the call light.

"Dean," Kat's eyes bulged with fear and she grabbed for his hand. "I can't breathe." Her chest heaved with effort and she struggled to sit up.

Dean raised the head of the bed to a sitting position.

Her grip tightened, and she trembled from the fever. She started coughing and couldn't catch her breath between bouts. "Dean," she panted, "help me. Don't. Let. Me. Die."

He watched, helpless, as her oxygen dropped to 85%, 82%, 79%. He cranked the oxygen up to six liters and hit the call light again, searching the drawers and cupboards in the room for an oxygen mask. Finding a non-rebreather mask in a pink tub in a cupboard, he ripped the package open, unhooked the nasal cannula from the wall and replaced it with the tubing to the mask, cranked the O2 up as high as it would go, took the cannula off Kat's face, and put the mask over her mouth and nose.

Holding her hand, Dean stared at the numbers on the monitor. 80%. 81%. 82%. That's as high as it got. He reached for the Code Blue button on the wall just as the nurse rushed back in, charge nurse right behind her.

"Dr. Bingham is on his way," the nurse said as she checked the oxygen mask Dean had put on Kat. "I called respiratory, too, they should be here any minute."

Kat coughed so hard she started gagging. Dean pulled the mask off in case she vomited, but she managed to hold it down. He moved the mask back over her face.

"Dean," the pleading in her muffled voice broke him. "Dean. Can't. Breathe."

79%

77%

74%

The respiratory therapist beat Dr. Bingham there by about two seconds. "Grab the crash cart!" He yelled at the charge nurse, as he lowered the head of the bed so Kat laid flat again.

Kat's eyes rolled in fear, her chest sucked in to her backbone with each attempt to breathe.

71%

Dr. Bingham hit the Code Blue button then pushed Dean out of the way as the charge nurse rolled the crash cart in. "Kat," the hospitalist said as he leaned over her. "I'm going to sedate you then put a breathing tube in your throat to help you breathe, then we'll move you up to the ICU."

"*Code blue, med/surg, room 351,*" was called over the hospital intercom.

Kat twisted around, flailing in the bed. "Dean." Another coughing fit.

This wasn't happening. This couldn't be happening.

"*Code blue, med/surg, room 351.*"

The bed was surrounded. Dean couldn't get to her. "I'm here, Kat. I won't leave you. I'm here." He backed up against the wall and watched as they worked on her.

The respiratory therapist replaced the non-rebreather mask with an ambu bag, pumping oxygen into her lungs each time she took a breath.

Dr. Bingham broke the crash cart open and grabbed the intubation kit from one of the drawers, opening it on the metal stand next to him. "Prepare to give twelve milligrams of Etomidate followed by eighty-five milligrams of Succs." He turned to the respiratory therapist. "Darin, hyperoxygenate her."

The ER doctor, Dr. Jasper ran into the room in response to the Code Blue, his face losing all color when his eyes met Dean's. He took in the controlled chaos in the room and said to the hospitalist, "What do you need me to do?"

"Get the bed in position."

Dr. Jasper unlocked the brakes and pulled the foot of the bed toward him, making room for Dr. Bingham to position himself at the head, then raised the whole bed up to make it easier to work on her. Darin stopped bagging long enough to remove the headboard from the bed.

"Meds are ready," the charge nurse called.

Another woman in scrubs that Dean vaguely recognized from the ER rushed in, looked around, and held her hand out to the charge nurse. "I'll record."

The charge nurse handed her a clipboard from the top of the crash cart.

Dr. Bingham snapped the laryngoscope open, the light turning on when it locked into place. He opened the ET tube package and laid the tube on the metal stand. "Give the Etomidate," he said.

The charge nurse attached a syringe to the IV line and kinked the tubing above it. "Giving twelve milligrams of Etomidate," she said as she pushed the plunger.

"Dean…" the muffled cry was barely audible above the noise in the room.

"I love you, Kat." Tears flooded from his eyes. He wrapped his arms around his torso and doubled over, gasping for breath between sobs. This couldn't be happening.

"Give the succs." Dr. Bingham's voice sounded far away, like it was under water. Under the ocean.

"Giving eighty-five milligrams of succs."

Not. Happening.

Dean looked up in time to see the hospitalist slide the endotracheal tube along the laryngoscope and into Kat's trachea. "No." Dean's throat closed as the horrors of the past collided with the nightmare of the present. Kat's lifeless body interposed over the serial killer standing above him holding an ET tube with a maniacal grin. Dean grabbed the back of the chair he stood next to, black spots floated in his sight as he fought to inhale past his collapsed trachea… As he fought to stay in the here and now instead of being dragged back to the abandoned jail.

With a gasp, Dean forced his throat open and gulped in a breath. Kat was all that mattered. He'd go back to that jail, back to Carter Ridge and his scalpel and torture, he would willingly give his life, if it would save Kat. He shoved the past away and straightened up.

Dr. Bingham held his stethoscope to Kat's chest as Darin pumped the bag, now attached to the ET tube. "It's in," the doctor said. "Secure the tube, start a propofol drip, and let's get her up to the ICU. Order a portable chest x-ray for when we get up there to check tube placement."

Dean looked up at the pulse oximeter. 92%. The boa constrictor wrapped around his chest relaxed just a little. He slumped against the wall, missing the chair as he slid to the floor, head in his hands.

TWENTY ONE

Rubbing his temples, Dean paced the hallway outside the ICU. His head pounded, and if they didn't let him in to see Kat soon, he might just kick the doors in. She'd deteriorated so fast. There had to be something more he could do.

He grabbed his phone from his pocket to check the time, remembering only when he saw a message from Tracey that she'd promised to send him the list of items confiscated from Andrew Matheson's home lab. Dean came to a dead stop and unlocked his phone, punching a finger at the message icon.

Four pictures of handwritten notes from Fitzpatrick's small spiral notebook popped up on the screen. Dean zoomed in on the first one, reading the list. Then the second. The third. And finally the fourth.

It wasn't there.

He looked at the lists again, slower this time, swearing under his breath. He called Tracey.

"What's up, Dean?" a sleepy Chief of Police answered.

"It isn't on the list." He knew he wasn't making any sense, but his head hurt, and his mind was firing a million thoughts per second, and Kat... Kat was dying. "The thing he sprayed her with, I don't think you got it."

"Slow down, Dr. Graves. We got everything we thought was pertinent to the investigation."

"Well, you missed something." Dean rolled his shoulders and forced himself to stop being such a jackass. "I'm sorry, I didn't mean to snap at you. But I need to go to Matheson's lab. Right now."

"Dean, it's late, and we were thorough in our search—"

"Tracey," he interrupted a little too loudly. Softening his voice, he repeated, "Tracey. Please. I'm not doubting your thoroughness, but I'm not sure your detectives would know what to look for."

She sighed. "Can it wait until morning? I sent Davis and Fitzpatrick home for the night—the overtime this month is outrageous."

"No." Dean spoke through clenched teeth. "It cannot wait. Tracey, I swear on all that is holy that I will go there by myself if I have to. I will cross through the police tape and break out a window. And I will be leaving the hospital in fifteen minutes to head over—"

"Dr. Graves," Tracey's tone was stern but resigned, "you will not step foot inside that house alone." She growled out a sigh. "I'll meet you there. Wait for me before you so much as open your car door." She hung up.

An ICU tech opened the doors into the unit and looked at him. "Are you with Katherine Flanagan?"

"Yes."

"You can come in now."

The tech led Dean to Kat's bedside. He held her hand and watched the rise and fall of her chest in time with the whooshing of the ventilator. "Kat." His voice broke. "I'm so sorry. I have to leave for a little while, but I won't be long. It's important. I wouldn't leave your side if it wasn't." He kissed her damp forehead. "I'll be back."

—⋀—

Even though Chief Billings had told him not to step outside his car until she arrived, he paced the length of it, glowering at the scientist's house, fists clamped tight at his sides, while he waited for her. The dark windows taunted him, a dim streetlamp reflecting off the largest one as if winking at him. Or beckoning.

Looking down the street in the direction he knew she'd be coming from, Dr. Graves mumbled, "It's about time," when Tracey's Jeep turned onto the street.

She parked behind his car and walked over to him with a scowl. "Come on. Let's get this over with."

Dr. Graves handed her an N-95 mask and donned his own, tightening the straps so it fit snug.

The neatly mown lawn, porch swing, and white window shutters looked like any other in the neighborhood, making Dr. Graves wonder at how one never knew what went on behind closed doors. How someone made up of nothing but pure evil could put on such a normal façade, living amongst average people who were just trying to live a normal life.

Chief Billings stomped around back to a set of cement stairs leading down to an outside entrance to the basement. She handed him her flashlight while she unlocked the padlock installed earlier by the police.

Dr. Graves looked around the large space after Chief Billings flipped the lights on. Kat hadn't exaggerated about the extent of equipment in this home lab. Sturdy stainless-steel tables ran the length of the room, and shelves hung from every available space on the walls. A tissue culture hood stood across the room from the large refrigerator and freezer.

He concentrated on the tables. As Kat had described it, that's where Matheson had been standing when he sprayed her. It appeared that the detectives had taken all the beakers and glass tubes from the equipment there. Dr Graves walked slowly, examining each piece of equipment with the trained eye of a pathologist. Kat had said Matheson pulled a length of tubing from a "machine." Which of these machines would have contained a concentrated dose of the bacteria?

Not the centrifuge—Kat would know what that was, plus the type of tube she'd described wouldn't be connected to it. Not the microscope. Not likely the droplet PCR system, though he inspected it closely for any rubberized or silicone tubing, finding none.

Dr. Graves continued his slow march, in awe at the high-level equipment Matheson had somehow amassed. Rounding the end of the tables, he started up the other side, pausing in front of a bead beater. It didn't appear to have been used recently. The cord was neatly folded and tied with a zip tie, unplugged from a power source.

"This could be it," he muttered, stopping in front of an instrument about the size of a small microwave.

"What is that?" Chief Billings stepped up beside him.

He flinched, having forgotten she was there. "It's a microfluidizer."

"Uh huh," the chief uttered. "That's what I was thinking."

Catching the sarcasm in her tone he glanced at her then back at the microfluidizer. He didn't have the patience to give a lengthy explanation. He pulled on a pair of gloves from a box on a shelf behind them and turned back to the equipment. "It's used to process gram-negative organisms—like *Legionella*." He unhooked a small length of tubing hidden within some of the components and held it out to her. "Do you have an evidence bag to put this in?" Now that he'd seen the short length of the tube, he no longer thought it was the right one, but it might prove to be important, anyway.

"Of course I do." Chief Billings pulled a bag out of her fanny-pack and held it open for him.

As he dropped the tubing in, another piece of equipment caught his eye, and he quickly moved over to it. "This is a chemostat...a bioreactor."

"We took all the glass vials off that thing. There were small droplets of fluid still inside some of them."

"Good. This is it." Dr. Graves disconnected several lengths of tubing from the machine, the longest of which would easily have stretched far enough to spray fluid at someone walking close by. He placed the tubing inside a second evidence bag held out by the chief. "Get that to the crime lab ASAP."

"Yes, sir. I'll drop it off there on my way home." Tracey touched his arm and looked into his eyes. "We *are* leaving now, right?"

Dean nodded. But he wasn't going home. He headed straight back to the hospital.

TWENTY TWO

Between the dim overhead lighting, flashing lights on the machines, and constant beeping of monitors, Dean's headache had gone from barely tolerable to excruciating. He couldn't concentrate—and he needed to concentrate now more than ever.

He looked over at Kat, hooked up to machines, a tube in her throat helping her breathe. *Breathing for her.* His headache was nothing compared to what she was going through. Even though she was sedated, she seemed unsettled. There was a crease in her brow that wasn't usually there, her muscles twitched frequently. Dean snaked his hand through the bed's side rail and stroked her arm. Her skin was so hot. "I'm here, Kat," he whispered over and over.

Dr. Shah had met them in the ICU last night, but he didn't have any new answers. He'd encouraged Dean to go home and get some rest, but once he saw how determined Dean was to stay, he stopped trying.

Now it was the middle of the night and the acetaminophen Dr. Shah had given him had long worn off. He rubbed his temples then turned back to his laptop screen, working the mouse with one hand while comforting Kat with the other.

Dean logged into his work email and noticed his contact at the CDC had emailed him back. His response was simple: *Andrew Matheson is BAD NEWS, stay as far away from him as possible.* Too late.

Tapping his fingers on the metal stand, Dean considered ways he might find more information about Andrew Matheson. What was the connection with the showerheads? How would an unemployed scientist have access to new bathroom fixtures or manufacturers? Making it more confusing was the knowledge that the showerheads came from different, unrelated companies.

Well, Dean didn't know much about social media, but he knew you could find connections there without too much trouble. And he had to start somewhere. He didn't have his own profile on any social media sites, but years ago, before Kat came along, one of his assistants had insisted that the city morgue needed a "Facebook presence" and had created a profile. Needless to say, it had been inactive ever since that employee quit. Dean logged in and searched "Andrew Matheson."

Several profiles with that name popped up. He scrolled down and stopped on one whose profile picture was a biohazard sign. He clicked it and scrolled through the posts. Nothing had been posted for years, but he knew it was the right profile when a photo of a younger Andrew in a cap and gown in front of the iconic Harvard Memorial Hall building appeared.

Dean clicked on the "About" tab. There wasn't much information there, two former workplaces were listed, but nothing recent. He clicked on the "Family and Relationship" tab, curious about the mad-scientist's family. There were only two profiles listed there: both cousins. Dean opened the profile for the first one, Taylor Rodden. This account was active, he'd posted something just yesterday. Dean leaned forward as he noticed the guy's listed occupation: Owner/Operator of Georgia Rain – Gasket & Seal Manufacturer.

Opening another internet tab, he typed in "Georgia Rain Gaskets" and opened the website. This was it. This was the connection, he realized, as photos of showerheads and other bathroom fixtures flashed across the screen.

It was just after four A.M. And Dean didn't care if he woke up the whole Augusta Police Department. Standing, he leaned over Kat, kissed her forehead, and said, "I'll be right back."

He exited the ICU and stood in the deserted hallway to make his phone call. A groggy, irritable Chief Billings answered, "This better be good."

"Tracey, it's Dean. I know how he got the bacteria into the showerheads."

"Hold on," a more awake Tracey said. Sheets rustled and a mattress creaked, a grunt from Tracey as she stood, footsteps, and then a door opening and closing. "Okay, Dean, whatcha got?"

"Andrew Matheson has a cousin that owns a gasket manufacturing company."

"So?"

"They manufacture gaskets that go inside showerheads."

Silence from Tracey as the information sunk in. Then, "Well I'll be damned. How'd you find that out in the middle of the night sittin' in a hospital room?"

"The power of social media. The company's name is Georgia Rain, and the owner, Andrew's cousin, is Taylor Rodden."

"Text it to me. I'm gonna call my detectives and then get dressed. Good job, Dean." She ended the call before he could tell her to keep him updated. But she would. She always did.

⎯⋀⎯

Two hours later, Dean was jolted awake by his phone vibrating across the metal mayo stand. His arm was asleep from remaining in one position while holding Kat's hand for hours as he dozed in the uncomfortable reclining chair next to her. He grabbed for the phone with his other hand, saw that it was Chief Billings, and answered, "Tracey, what did you find out?"

"Well, an early morning visit by two detectives wasn't what poor Mr. Rodden was expecting. Needless to say, he was in complete shock when they explained why they were there. He paid Mr. Matheson to design a new gasket for him, solely for showerheads, after Matheson was 'let go' from his job at the CDC. Hang on, I gotta get some coffee." Her muffled voice came through the phone as she ordered.

Dean stood and ran his hand through his messy hair, then rubbed the two-day stubble on his cheeks. Coffee sounded good. He would definitely need some to get through this day.

"Okay, you still there?" Tracey asked.

"Where else would I be?" Dean said.

"So, anyway, the cousin said he at first just offered Matheson a job in the manufacturing plant, but Matheson came to him with a new idea for these gaskets—like a new material or something. He insisted on being the one to make the sheets of material for the machines to cut or press or whatever—the detectives kinda lost me with the technical stuff."

"And you're sure the cousin didn't know what he was doing?"

"Davis and Rodriguez both swore that he acted like he had no idea. He invited them into his house while he printed up a complete list of all the companies that have purchased the new gaskets, then he met them at his warehouse and gave them some of the gaskets and the sheets of material."

"We need to alert the CPSC. They need to issue a recall immediately," Dean said.

"CPSC?"

"The Consumer Product Safety Commission, Tracey! How do you not know that?"

"Chill out, Dr. Graves. Why would I know that? I'm not usually in the business of investigating tainted products."

"Sorry. I'm a little on edge."

"A little?" She snorted. "I'll get someone on that recall right now." She hung up.

The morning shift arrived and kicked Dean out while they completed a bedside report. He went in search of coffee. A sympathetic housekeeper gave him directions to a coffee cart set up in the main lobby, telling him that the cafeteria coffee was disgusting. His nose led him right to it as soon as he stepped off the elevator.

—ᐱ—

DEAN PACED in the small area at the foot of Kat's hospital bed, both hands pulling at his hair, as Dr. Shah, an ICU resident, a pulmonologist, two nurses, and a respiratory therapist stood around her discussing what to do next. She'd worsened over the last hour. They'd increased the settings on the ventilator as high as they dared, explaining to Dean that any higher and they risked further damaging her lungs or even causing a pneumothorax.

Exhaustion and worry made it difficult for Dean to keep track of the conversation, with words like PEEP, tidal volume, time ratio, and ARDS breaking through. He knew those terms, but in his current state of mind he couldn't process their meaning as it pertained to Kat. The pulmonologist suggested ECMO and Dean's over stimulated brain translated it in slow motion: extra...corporeal... membrane...oxygenation.

"Dr. Graves, what do you think?" Dr. Shah asked.

Dean flinched, then looked at Dr. Shah with pleading eyes. "Romit," he grabbed his friend's arm, "just do whatever it takes to keep her alive. Please. I'm going to go find a cure."

TWENTY THREE

Dean drove straight to the crime lab and, ignoring the protests of the receptionist and the security guard, pushed his way into the lab.

"Dr. Graves, can I help you?"

Spinning toward the voice, Dean recognized Sara Lamb, a forensic scientist that had been employed there since before he started with the city. They had crossed paths frequently over the years. "Sara, I need a sample from the Matheson case, the *Legionella* case."

"Dean... I can't just hand you a sample from—"

"Sara, please. Kat's dying" his voice broke, and he dropped his face into his hands, no longer in control of his emotions. A mournful sob that couldn't have come from him, issued from deep inside his core.

Arms wrapped around him, comforting him in a warm embrace. He sobbed into the small woman's hair for several minutes before realizing he was wasting precious time. He straightened, and Sara dropped her arms and stepped back to look at him.

Dean wiped his face and took a steadying breath, but his voice still came out broken, desperate. "Sara, I need a sample. I'll take it straight to Atlanta. I need to find something that will stop this shit from killing her."

Mild surprise registered in Sara's eyes. She put her hands on her hips and tilted her head, narrowing her eyes as she considered. She nodded, as if coming to a conclusion. She looked at the only other person in the lab and said, "Tanner, go to lunch."

He looked up from a computer. "Okay, let me just—"

"Now," Sara said.

The tech nodded, locked the screen on his computer, and left, looking behind him once as he reached the door.

Sara sighed, walked over to a large stainless-steel warmer, and typed in a code to open the door. She reached in and grabbed a petri dish from a stack of four and handed it to Dean. "I'm going to have to do paperwork for this petri dish that became compromised when I *dropped* it. And I hate paperwork, Dean."

"Thank you. I owe you...anything. I'll do anything to pay you back."

The lines on her face smoothed, and she touched his arm. "No need for that. This is a sample directly from the tubing your Kat was sprayed with. I plated it yesterday as soon as it came in and it has already grown, as you can see."

"But, don't you need it—"

She stopped him with a shake of her head. "You know me better than that. I have three others from the same source." She pulled a small insulated bag from a cupboard and handed it to him. "Put it in there, that should keep it warm on your way to Atlanta."

—⋀—

"I'LL GET everything ready for when you get here, Dr. Graves," Dr. Jason Michaels said.

Dr. Graves sighed in relief. The Georgia Department of Health director hadn't asked any questions, he'd just agreed to help.

Dean stopped for gas and grabbed a donut and a bottle of water—two things he rarely consumed—because he hadn't eaten since early yesterday morning. At the register, he impulsively threw in two small bottles of some kind of energy drink. It wouldn't do to fall asleep and crash on his way to Atlanta. He didn't have time for that.

—⋀—

THE HASTILY ASSEMBLED team of doctors and microbiologists, including Dr. Graves, Dr. Michaels, and Dr. Liz Allen, worked late into the night to come up with an unconventional treatment plan that they believed had a good chance of fighting off the manmade super-bacteria.

Dr. Graves called Dr. Shah at 4:12 A.M., waking him up. "Dr. Shah, it's Dr. Graves. We have a treatment plan for Kat so splash some water on your face or something to make sure you're fully awake."

"I'm awake, Dean. Just let me grab a pen and paper so I can take notes." Shuffling footsteps, a drawer opening, rummaging, drawer closing, and then, "Okay, go ahead."

Again, Dean was thankful for a friend that didn't ask a lot of unnecessary questions during a time sensitive emergency. "This bacteria is super strong." Extreme fatigue reduced his choice of words to the most basic. "Attacking it passively with just IV antibiotics isn't working, so we need to attack it directly, at the source, in the lungs."

"Okay, that makes sense. I'm with you so far."

"Continue the IV azithromycin, levofloxacin, and rifampin, but add nebulized gentamicin and ceftazidime. And, I know this might sound odd, but nebulized amphotericin."

"Have you found a fungal component?" Dr. Shah sounded a little surprised by the suggestion.

"We haven't been able to isolate a fungal component yet, but we're ninety-percent sure it's there. He somehow hid it in one of the *Legionella* serogroups. I don't know, I'm too tired to grasp the science of it, but the microbiologists here are convinced that's the case."

"I'll have to figure out the dosages. Nebulizing those drugs is an off-label use."

"Just talk to the pediatric pulmonologists—they have likely used all three for their Cystic Fibrosis patients. Start the nebulized meds immediately."

"I'll call it in as soon as I have dosages and administration instructions. Then I'll head straight to the hospital to observe Katherine's condition."

"Thank you, Ramit. I'll be there in about two hours." Dean ended the call and rubbed his eyes, dropping into the nearest chair.

"You are not driving yourself back to Augusta tonight," Liz said.

He leaned back, tilting his head against the wall, eyes closed. "I have to, Liz."

"Matt and I already worked it out. I'll drive you in your car and Matt will follow in my car. I'm tired, but I've only been up since seven yesterday morning—and I took a nap while y'all were doing the scientist stuff. You've been awake for who knows how long and you look like you're ready to collapse."

"What about your kids?" Dean asked, eyes still closed.

"We have a nanny, my eighteen-year-old niece is staying with us for the summer."

Dean nodded. "'Kay, but let's get on the road."

"Matt should be here any minute."

―⋀―

DEAN LAID the passenger seat back and was asleep before they even pulled out of the parking lot.

TWENTY FOUR

"I got him, Dr. Graves," Detective Isabella Rodriguez said. "I wanted to tell you in person."

They stood in the ICU waiting room Thursday morning. It had been three days since anyone had seen Andrew Matheson. Three days since he'd sprayed a deadly bacterial concoction in Kat's face. "Detective, thank you. I...where?" Dean had gotten a little sleep in the recliner next to Kat's bed last night, but it in no way made up for the lack of sleep over the previous days.

"First, how is Miss Flanagan?"

"She's stable. She's off ECMO but still on the ventilator. They've been able to lower the settings a little."

Rodriguez nodded. "I'm glad to hear that, sir."

"So, you got him? And he's alive?"

"Yes, sir, to both questions. I was listening to radio traffic last night, 'cause I couldn't sleep." She shrugged. "And I heard a call come in about an illegally parked car that turned out to be registered to Matheson. When I heard the location, I had a hunch. I remembered you talking about how this bacteria is transmitted by water, and his car was parked on Central Avenue. I looked up the location and realized it was near one of the water treatment plants."

Dr. Graves whipped his head up, alarm causing an adrenaline spike. "He was trying to contaminate our drinking water." It wasn't a question but a statement of certainty. "Did he succeed?"

"No, sir. I radioed dispatch and headed down there. Two uniformed officers met me in the parking lot, and we split up to search for him. I figured he'd be wherever the clean water was stored, so I pulled up a picture of the plant and started there."

"Good thinking. That's exactly where I would have started looking."

Her mouth quirked up at the corners briefly. "Well, for a scientific genius, he sure doesn't have much common sense. The clean water tanks are underground. I caught him digging above where the tanks' approximate location is. He'd managed to dig down about three feet—not sure what his plans were once he reached the tanks or pipes, he didn't have any other equipment besides the shovel. He had a bag full of vials laying a few feet away from him. I moved between him and the bag before he noticed me, pulled my sidearm and pointed it at him, and said 'drop the shovel, dumbass.'" A sheepish grin flashed on her face and she shrugged. "Excuse the language."

Dean smiled for the first time in days. "No need to apologize. It's a fitting nick-name for him. Did he resist?"

"Of course he did. Or he tried to. It took him several tries to get out of the hole he'd dug himself into. I called the uniforms to my location, but by the time they got there I'd thrown the suspect to the ground and had him handcuffed." She gestured at the dirt and grass stains on the knees of her pants.

"Excellent work."

"Anyway, he's locked up now. The vials of his superbug are tucked safely away at the crime lab. And I'm going home to shower and take a nap."

"Detective Rodriguez, thank you for your diligence. And thank you for coming here to tell me you caught the bastard."

Her eyebrows shot up at his use of a curse word, but she smiled and nodded.

⎯⋀⎯

Forehead creased in concentration, Dr. Shah scrolled through Kat's electronic medical record at the bedside computer. After signing out of the chart, he turned to Dean, arms folded, flipping a pen against his arm.

"What?" Dean asked with a death grip on the siderail of the bed. Stomach acid boiled in his esophagus, burning holes through the tissue, he was sure.

"We seem to have hit a plateau. She's been on the inhaled medication for thirty-six hours now, and after an initial improvement in her condition, we haven't been able to turn down the ventilator settings for the last sixteen hours."

Dean looked down at his hands, knuckles white. The flexor carpi ulnaris muscles of both arms ached and twitched, yet he couldn't relax his grip. "What...what does that mean? What else can we do?"

"The pulmonologist thinks it's the fungal aspect that is holding up the progress. Fungal infections are complicated to treat under the best of circumstances—and not knowing exactly what we're dealing with here is making it more difficult." Dr. Shah walked over and stood next to Dean. "We need to know what that fungus is, Dean."

"I know. The CDC hasn't been able to isolate it yet because of the way it's embedded in one of the bacterial strains. It's proving difficult."

Dr. Shah wagged his head. "Well, let me know as soon as they figure it out."

In his head, Dean finished Dr. Shah's statement with, *before it's too late to save her.* As Dr. Shah left the room, Dean slumped into the chair next to Kat's bed, dropping his head into his hands. They may never figure out what the fungus was. What if it was a combination of fungi like the new *Legionella* bacteria Matheson created? Or he somehow generated one with an impermeable outer membrane?

His head spun with every possible—and until now impossible—modification the scientist could have carried out. The only way to know for sure at this point, was to go to the source.

That's what he'd do. Dr. Graves stood and grabbed his phone from the bedside table, stopping briefly to squeeze Kat's hand before leaving the room. He called Chief Billings' cell as he hurried to the elevator and punched the down arrow.

"Dean—"

He cut her off. "I need to speak with Matheson. I'm on my way to the jail now, it should take me twenty minutes to get there. Do whatever you have to do to ensure I'll be allowed to question him when I get there."

"Whoa, hold on a minute. What—"

"Tracey, I don't have time for any bureaucratic bullshit," his voice wavered, "Kat's life is on the line."

"I thought she was doin' better?"

Exiting the elevator, he swept through a group of people carrying "Get Well Soon" balloons and rushed out the hospital entrance toward the parking lot. "She's no longer improving. We need a bit of information only Matheson can give us." He reached his car. "Gotta go. Please help me with this." He ended the call before she could answer.

⎯⋀⎯

DURING THE TWENTY-MINUTE DRIVE, Dr. Graves contemplated how to approach Andrew Matheson. There was no doubt in his mind that the scientist was a narcissist. Playing on his ego, his obvious need to be recognized for his achievements—both real and imagined—was likely the best way to get the information out of him.

He parked under a lamppost that wasn't illuminated yet, but would be by the time he left the jail. He read the text message Chief Billings had sent while he drove: *It's a good thing we're friends and I trust you. The detectives will meet you there. They have to be present while you question the suspect. Call me when you're done.*

"Suspect," he shook his head. There was absolutely no doubt that

Matheson was the one who'd committed these acts of bioterrorism. It really irked Dr. Graves that they still had to call him anything but murderer.

One of the city's unmarked police cars pulled into the parking spot next to him. He got out of his car and waited for the detectives to join him. Nodding to Detective Rodriguez as she exited the driver's side, he felt a slight sense of relief that she would join him. She seemed to understand his penchant for solemnity and order in times such as this. Dr. Graves wasn't as pleased to see Detective Davis step out of the passenger side.

"Graves," the detective said, "I hope you don't plan on taking too long in there. I have a recliner and a cold beer waiting for me at home."

Dr. Graves swallowed down a flash of anger.

"It's *Doctor* Graves, you neanderthal." Detective Rodriguez beat him to it.

"Thank you, detective." Dr. Graves tilted his head toward her, then glared at her partner. "And it will take however long it takes to get the information I need. The information *Kat* needs."

"Then let's go get it, doctor," Rodriguez said.

Following behind the detectives, Dr. Graves reviewed his plan, too worried about Kat and furious at Matheson to feel nervous about the coming confrontation.

At the front desk, the corrections officer asked for their IDs then buzzed them in. "The prisoner is waiting for you in interview room one."

Dr. Graves rolled his shoulders and stood tall as the detectives led him to the interview room. A quiet intrusion prodded his thoughts, a glimpse of a memory about the last time he'd been inside a jail setting. His steps faltered, he stopped and closed his eyes, tightening his jaw, and thought, *Get out of my head, Ridge. I need to be focused. For Kat.*

"Everything okay, Dr. Graves?" Detective Rodriguez asked.

He opened his eyes and nodded.

As they entered the room, Dr. Graves' eyes flicked from the uniformed guard standing against the wall behind the prisoner, to Matheson, wearing an orange jumpsuit, sitting handcuffed to a table in the center of the small room.

Dr. Graves sat in the chair straight across from the murderous scientist, leaving the chairs to either side of him for the detectives. He stared straight at Matheson's eyes, wanting to swat the smug look off his face.

"Dr. Graves, how is Miss Flanagan doing? I heard she became ill shortly after her visit to my lab." Matheson shook his head and frowned.

Clenching his fists under the table, Dr. Graves forced a smile. "She is doing much better since I figured out the complexities of your designer bacteria and its susceptibilities."

Matheson's right eye twitched so minutely, Dr. Graves doubted anyone but him noticed. He'd struck a nerve.

"Is that so?" The murderer leaned back against his chair. "And... what are these susceptibilities?"

"I assumed you would have figured that all out before releasing it." Dr. Graves shrugged. "That's what *I* would have done."

With a glance at the detectives, Matheson said, "Well, *if* I had been the one to create and release such a deadly bacteria, I most definitely would have had the cure figured out beforehand. I'm just curious to know what a genius such as yourself discovered."

"Just a cocktail of inhaled medications, the specifics aren't important here." Dr. Graves leaned forward and whispered, "I wonder, though, how long it took *you* to figure out the right combination and delivery of the drugs. The intellectually competitive side of me needs to know if the eight hours it took me to come up with the cure was on par with your genius." He sat back, keeping his face neutral. "Of course it was very helpful to have samples directly from your home lab to work with. Amazing set-up you had there."

Anger flashed in Matheson's eyes, and he pitched forward in his chair. "Had? Past tense? What have they done to my lab?"

"Oh, I'm afraid it's all been packed away as evidence. It's a pity that all that high-tech equipment will eventually be sold off piece by piece to the highest bidder."

Matheson closed his eyes and drew in a breath. He relaxed back against the chair again and crossed his legs, trying to fold his arms across his chest, but the shackles restraining him to the table prevented it. His jaw tightened, and he laid his shaking hands back on the table. "What are you really after, Dr. Graves? A man with your genius must know that I would have known the cure before even developing the disease."

Dr. Graves had to tread lightly here. Had to bring it up in the right way. Had to use Matheson's ego against him. And he couldn't let on that he didn't know what the fungal component was. "Yes, I expected as much. My curiosity has gotten the better of me, I'm afraid." He placed his right hand on the table and drummed his fingers against the hard surface to hide the tremor his anger was causing. "None of us—myself nor your former colleagues at the CDC —have been able to quite figure out how you embedded the fungal spores into the new *Legionella* strain you created. I mean, I knew you were intelligent, but, for instance, how did you account for the difference in pH preferences?"

With a sneer, Matheson spat, "Those idiots at the CDC wouldn't know a fungus from a bacteria from a virus. They never appreciated my genius. Every single one of them was jealous of me."

"Some people just don't understand innovation on the biological front, I guess." He'd have to rinse his mouth out with chlorhexidine after all the BS spewing out of it. "They didn't even seem curious about the fungus. They just wanted to focus on the new strain."

The muscles of Matheson's face smoothed out, and the earlier smugness returned to his demeanor. "I knew that would stump them. Idiots don't even know the difference between prokaryotes and eukaryotes."

"Well, you have to admit that not just any scientist would have been able to do what you did." *Because no sane microbiologist would want to,* he wanted to add. It was getting increasingly difficult to continue to stroke this maniac's ego. Dr. Graves' temples throbbed with the effort to keep his cool.

"True." Matheson smiled, a sociopathic twisting of his lips, and leaned in conspiratorially, whispering, "The full process is a trade secret, but I can tell you the essence of it. Obviously most fungal cells are too big to embed into a bacterial cell." He paused and pointed a finger at Dr. Graves. "But the conidia fit lengthwise quite nicely. And implanting it between the capsid and cell wall of the *Legionella* organism makes it very difficult to find. It won't even grow when cultured because it's hidden behind the protective capsid." He narrowed his eyes, frowning. "How *did* you figure it out?"

Dr. Graves tapped a finger to the side of his head, hoping to avoid answering the question. "Great minds think alike." His next question was the important one. The only reason he'd come. He had to tread carefully. "How did you decide which fungus to use?"

Matheson's demeanor changed back to one of arrogance. "*Blastomyces dermatitidis* was the perfect—"

"Got it!" Dr. Graves stood and looked at the uniformed guard. "You may take this narcissistic psychopath back to his cell, where I hope he rots slowly over the next several decades."

The detectives hurried to catch up to him as he rushed from the interview room. "That was spectacular," Detective Rodriguez said.

"That was confusing," Davis muttered.

"Why, Detective Davis," Dr. Graves said as he continued to speed-walk out of the building, "I would think that a card-carrying member of MENSA such as yourself would have easily kept up with the conversation."

Rodriguez guffawed as Davis sputtered an incoherent response.

"Thanks for your help, detectives." Dr. Graves got into his car, locked the doors, and called Dr. Shah's cell.

"Dr. Graves—"

"Ramit," he interrupted. "It's Blastomycosis. Change to parenteral liposomal amphotericin B and add IV itraconazole. Sorry, I know you already know the treatment. I'm just anxious to get it started on her. I'll be there in twenty minutes."

"I'm on it, Dean. See you soon."

TWENTY FIVE

The health commissioner had brought in a temporary pathologist and autopsy assistant to cover for him and Kat after Dr. Graves insisted he was not going to leave Kat's bedside until she was able to walk out of the hospital on her own two feet. He just hoped they weren't making a mess of things. He really hated it when other people messed with his morgue.

Dean rarely got emails that weren't spam or junk mail on his personal email account, so he rarely checked it. Boredom got to him as he sat watching Kat's chest move up and down with each assisted breath, so he logged into his email. At the top of the inbox was a message from the rental agency he'd reserved a cottage from for this weekend. He'd forgotten all about the romantic getaway he'd planned. He looked over at Kat and rubbed her arm, whispering, "When you're all better, we'll plan an even better trip. Anywhere you want to go."

He emailed the company, explaining the situation, hoping to be able to cancel the reservation without having to pay. But it really didn't matter. It was just money.

Leaning his head back, he closed his eyes, just for a minute...

"Dr. Graves?" The ICU resident shook him by the shoulder.

Dean sprang forward in a panic, nearly toppling out of the chair. In the moments it took him to recognize his surroundings, his eyes saw the abandoned jail cell, a dangling flashlight, a murderer's gleeful face. Now standing, he bent, resting his hands on his knees as he took a few deep breaths, trying to slow his racing heart.

"Umm...sorry... I—"

"You shouldn't wake me up by touching me," Dr. Graves said in a growling voice. He pushed on his knees and stood straight. One look into the resident's wide eyes, and Dr. Graves' frustration turned to mercy. "It's okay. You didn't know. I have...I had some trauma a while back, and I, well, I just don't wake up smoothly sometimes."

"Trauma is an understatement." Dr. Shah stood just inside the doorway. "Next time, just call his name from here."

"Duly noted," the resident said, nodding.

Dean looked around at the assembled medical team then gave himself whiplash as he turned to check on Kat. "What's going on?"

"She's fine, Dr. Graves," the nurse assured him—a different nurse than he'd last seen.

Looking up at the clock, he realized he'd been asleep for several hours, long enough for shift change to have occurred. This was the night nurse. He rubbed the hair on his face that he could no longer call just stubble.

"It's good news, Dean," Dr. Shah said. "She's been on the inhaled medications for over sixty hours now and on the new fungal medications for twenty-four hours, and we've seen marked improvement in her lung elasticity, her blood gasses, and her chest x-ray. We've been weening her ventilator settings over the last twelve hours, she passed the spontaneous breathing trial, and we are confident she is ready to be extubated."

"You're sure?" His voice was barely above a whisper. Less than two days ago he'd thought he was going to lose her. He stepped to her bedside and took her hand, staring at her swollen face.

"As sure as we can be," the pulmonologist said.

"You can stay right here," the nurse patted his arm, "and hold her hand while we turn off the propofol. We stopped the midazolam earlier today, so she could wake up within minutes, or it could take hours."

Dr. Graves nodded, not trusting himself to speak.

The respiratory therapist and ICU doctor stood at her head,

equipment ready to reintubate if necessary. The nurse stopped the sedation and flushed the IV.

Dean stroked Kat's arm and face as he leaned close and whispered to her. "It's time to wake up, Kat. I want to see your beautiful brown eyes looking back at me. I love you."

She began to stir after only a few minutes. At the ten-minute mark she squeezed his hand and her eyes fluttered opened, spinning around in her head with panic until they landed on Dean.

"It's okay, Kat. You're okay."

"We're going to sit you up and get this tube out of your throat, Miss Flanagan," the nurse said as she raised the head of the bed.

The RT said, "I'm going to suction the tube and inside your mouth before we take it out." When he finished, he disconnected the ET tube from the ventilator and unfastened the tube holder, standing by with the suction catheter and oxygen.

"Okay, Miss Flanagan," the ICU doctor said, "when I say 'breathe' I want you to take a deep breath, and when you exhale, I'll remove the tube." He connected a syringe to the port to deflate the cuff holding the tube in place. "Okay, breathe." As she exhaled, he pulled back on the syringe's plunger to deflate the cuff, then smoothly removed the tube from her throat.

"Once more with the suction," the RT warned before inserting it into her mouth. When he pulled it out he instructed, "Now take a deep breath and cough up all that gunk in your throat."

Kat's cough was strong, and Dean didn't think he'd ever heard anything so wonderful. That is, until she stopped coughing, looked at him, and said, "You need a shave."

TWENTY SIX

Dean went home to shower and, yes, shave, and to check in on Hermione who was out of control with excitement to see him. The guilt at having to leave her at the neighbor's again brought his elation down just a little.

A floral shop caught his eye as he hurried back to the hospital, and he swerved into the parking lot on an unheard-of—for him—expedition into spontaneity.

Smiling at the tall glass vase sporting twenty artfully arranged sunflowers buckled into his passenger seat, Dean took in a deep breath. The subtle, earthy smell of the flowers lifted his spirits.

They'd moved Kat back to the medical floor late Saturday after she'd proved she could breathe on her own for over twenty-four hours. She still wore a nasal cannula around her beautiful face, with oxygen blowing into her nostrils at four liters per minute, but that was nothing compared to where he'd thought she was heading a few days ago.

He'd never in his life felt like skipping, but today, as he carried the vase full of Kat's favorite flowers into the hospital, and a smaller arrangement for the nurses, he had to remind himself that he was a grown man—a grown man who did not skip.

Stopping at the nurses' station, Dean smiled and handed the small vase of wildflowers to the clerk.

"Wow, Dr. Graves," a nurse that came up behind the clerk said, "y'all clean up nice."

The clerk cocked her head to the side and grinned. "I don't know, I kinda liked the grungy, disheveled, bearded Dr. Graves."

"Ladies," Chief Billings' voice broke through their flirtatious banter, "y'all can flirt and pay him compliments all you want, but y'all need to know two things: one, Dean Graves is taken—one-hundred-percent smitten with Miss Flanagan in that room down the hall; and two, he can no more pick up on ladies coming on to him than a rock can skip itself across a pond. Y'all are fighting a losing battle."

Heat flashed up his neck and into his cheeks. Of course, they were flirting. He wasn't completely oblivious. He shrugged and smiled before turning to greet Tracey. "Hey, chief. How'd she do while I was gone?"

As he walked with her back to Kat's room, the clerk's voice carried to them, "I almost like the backside view as much as the front."

It was like she wasn't even trying to keep her voice down! The heat in his cheeks flamed hotter as Tracey laughed.

The nurse responded, also not trying to speak quietly, "I agree it's a nice view, but those thick eyelashes, the baby blues, strong jaw..."

Dean sped up, nearly jogging down the hall to Kat's room while Tracey's laughter followed him. He burst through the door like Kramer in Seinfeld, bobbling the large vase.

"Dean!" Kat said. "You scared me!"

"I'm sorry, Kat." He looked behind him. "Those nurses scare *me!*"

The puzzled look on her face was adorable and made him forget all about the teasing women. He set the flowers on the nightstand next to the bed and kissed Kat on the forehead as Tracey laughed her way through the door.

"Those flowers are beautiful." Kat covered her mouth and coughed for several seconds. She raised an eyebrow. "Dean, why are you blushing and why is Tracey laughing?"

Dean just shook his head, choosing that moment to check the monitors and see how much oxygen Kat was on now. Down from four liters to two.

Chief Billings took the liberty of answering her question, though.

"Those nurses out there were flirting up a storm with your...*boss*." She chuckled. "He just doesn't know how to take it."

Kat smiled and straightened the covers over her lap. "Ahh, that explains it." She patted Dean's hand that rested on the bedrail. "That must have been terrifying for you."

How could he stop these two from tormenting him? He looked back at Kat, her chocolate-colored eyes still sunken and tired but gorgeous all the same. "Naw. I just couldn't wait to get back to you." He lifted her chin with a finger and kissed her chapped lips.

It was her turn to blush. "Dean, my breath probably smells like the yellow rubber this place tried to pass off as eggs this morning! At least let me brush my teeth and put some lip balm on before you kiss me."

Tracey stepped to the other side of Kat's bed. "I believe that's my cue to leave. You two lovebirds are nauseating." She touched Kat's arm and said, "Y'all keep getting better. I'll check in on you later."

"Thanks, Chief Billings," Kat said.

"Yes," Dean added, "thank you for staying with her while I went home and cleaned up."

"Yes, thank you." Kat rolled her eyes at him. "Even though I would have been fine by myself for an hour."

"Any time." The Chief of Police, Dean's friend, nodded.

"Oh, I meant to ask you," Dean said, "did you find anything useful on Matheson's laptop?"

Tracey's face lit up. "Did we ever! He might be a genius mad scientist, but his IT skills are severely lacking. He had a file labeled 'Master Plan' with all the details we'll need to put him away for life. You shoulda' seen his lawyer's face when the D.A. presented it to her!"

"Did his master plan include his motivation for doing this?" Dean asked.

Nodding, the chief said, "Besides the fact that he's a sociopath? Yeah. He wanted to be the hero, to show the CDC that they made a mistake when they fired him. His plan was to wait until there were multiple deaths and lots of media coverage, then worm his way into the investigation and 'find' the cure in record time, showing up all the doctors and scientists that had been working on it for weeks. My guess is that if Miss Flanagan here hadn't stumbled upon those showerhead diagrams, he would have presented you with the cure within a day of getting his hands on the water sample."

"That's basically what I would have guessed his motivation to be." Dean frowned, thinking about all the lives lost just to boost one man's ego. He looked at Kat as pressure built up behind his eyes, and thought, *and one very important life that was almost lost.*

"Yep, me too. Well, I've got a barbecue to go to, so I'll see you two later." Tracey shut the door behind her, leaving Dean and Kat alone.

"How are you feeling?" he asked.

She sighed and looked away, but not before tears sprang instantly to her eyes.

Dean took her hand and stood in silence while she composed herself.

A few moments later Kat wiped her face and looked at him. "I'm exhausted. I practically needed a wheelchair to get back to bed after going to the bathroom." She pointed to the door only a few feet from the foot of her bed.

"That's to be expected. Your lungs took a big hit, and it's going to take some time to regain normal capacity and function."

"I know...but Dr. Black, the pulmonologist, said it might take up to eighteen months or longer." She wiped at another escaped tear. "That's a long time."

Dean brought her hand to his lips and pressed them to it while brushing a strand of hair from her face with his other hand. "Kat, I almost lost you," his voice wavered and cracked like an adolescent boy's. He cleared his throat. "Eighteen months to heal is but a drop in the bucket compared to facing the rest of my life without you. I know you feel helpless right now and have a long road ahead of you, but I'm just so very grateful that you're still here to walk that road." He pressed her hand to his chest. "And I will not leave your side while you do."

She sniffled then coughed. When she caught her breath, she teased, "I suppose you *do* owe it to me."

Thinking about the days, the weeks, she'd spent nursing him back to health after...he shook his head. That was even before he'd confessed his feelings to her. She'd done everything in her power to help him heal, both physically and mentally, and she hadn't asked for anything in return. "I owe you everything, Kat. And I'd like to spend the rest of my life paying you back."

—⌁—

KAT WAS RELEASED from the hospital five days later with home oxygen and a reluctant acquiescence to stay at Dean's house while she recovered. The hospitalist had warned them both that she may have some memory loss and have a hard time concentrating for a while. She'd also told them that the muscle aches and weakness were normal and would get better with time.

Neither of them had brought up the trip they'd planned on taking together. Maybe Kat didn't remember, it *had* been discussed right before she got infected with a super-bacteria. And Dean didn't mention it because he didn't want Kat to feel pressured in any way.

He held her hand as they stood out on his patio while an overjoyed Hermione ran halfway into the yard and back again, wagging her tail and nuzzling first Dean and then Kat over and over.

"Dean Graves," Kat said, turning to face him, "you are the best man I've ever met. Thank you for loving me as much as I love you."

Before he could respond, she pulled his head down to meet her, and she kissed him. Her lips tasted of toothpaste and cherry flavored lip balm. And even with the oxygen tubing pressed between them, it was the most amazing kiss he'd ever had.

EPILOGUE

In a hurry to get home to Kat, who was still recovering from her brush with death, Dr. Graves almost let his office phone ring unanswered as he was stepping out the door. But his work ethic wouldn't let him ignore it. He sighed and trudged back to his desk.

"Dr. Graves," he said into the phone.

"Graves, this is Fitzpatrick."

"*Doctor* Graves, detective. What do you want?"

"Yeah, that's what I meant, Dr. Graves. We need your help. You know that murder we started investigating during your time off?"

"Yes, I am aware of it." The temporary medical examiner had done an adequate job with the autopsy.

"Well, we just got the DNA results back from what we suspect was the killer's blood, and we don't know what to make of it."

"Why? Is it alien DNA or something?" Dr. Graves quipped as he looked at his watch.

"Ha ha. Funny." Fitzpatrick snorted. "It's a perfect match for a man that's already in prison—a man who's been in prison for the last three years."

Interesting. Dr. Graves' genius brain started grinding out different scenarios that would make that possible. As much as he didn't want to get involved with another murderer, this was too intellectually stimulating to pass up. "Send me everything you've got. I'll take a look at it tomorrow." He hung up and hurried out the door. Even an evidentiary mystery of this magnitude wouldn't keep him at work late tonight. Kat and Hermione needed dinner, and after a long day away, Dr. Graves needed them.

ABOUT THE AUTHOR

Holli Anderson has a Bachelor's Degree in Nursing—which has nothing to do with writing, except maybe by adding some pretty descriptive injury and vomit scenes to her books. She discovered her joy of writing during a very trying period in her life when escaping into make-believe saved her. She enjoys reading any book she gets her hands on.

Along with her husband, Steve, and their four sons, she lives in Grantsville, Utah—the same small town in which she grew up.

This has been an
Immortal Production